||| ||| ||| ||| ||| ||| ||| ||| |||
☝ **W9-BVE-059**

"My son didn't see anything, Wade!" Kerri shouted.

"He dropped his skateboard and ran when the fire started. I went back for his board. That's all. You need to leave us alone."

There was no denying the fury in her voice, but Wade spotted more than anger in her eyes. He'd known her long enough to know she was bluffing. "You're lying."

"I will not let you drag my son into this. Is that understood? He saw nothing."

Wade sighed. "Someone was murdered, Kerri. The police have a lead on who did this, but they need a witness."

One of her auburn brows lifted. "Get out of my house."

"I'd never let anything happen to him. Or you." Wade stepped out onto the front step, tensing as the door slammed behind him. He'd give her this round, but if she thought she'd won the battle, Kerri had another thing coming....

Park Rapids
Area Library
5-08

5-48

KATHLEEN LONG

RELUCTANT WITNESS

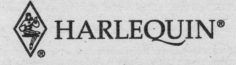

TORONTO • NEW YORK • LONDON
AMSTERDAM • PARIS • SYDNEY • HAMBURG
STOCKHOLM • ATHENS • TOKYO • MILAN • MADRID
PRAGUE • WARSAW • BUDAPEST • AUCKLAND

If you purchased this book without a cover you should be aware that this book is stolen property. It was reported as "unsold and destroyed" to the publisher, and neither the author nor the publisher has received any payment for this "stripped book."

As always, for Dan. Thank you for being
the most wonderful hero a girl could hope for.

ISBN-13: 978-0-373-22959-8
ISBN-10:   0-373-22959-3

RELUCTANT WITNESS

Copyright © 2006 by Kathleen Long

All rights reserved. Except for use in any review, the reproduction or utilization of this work in whole or in part in any form by any electronic, mechanical or other means, now known or hereafter invented, including xerography, photocopying and recording, or in any information storage or retrieval system, is forbidden without the written permission of the publisher, Harlequin Enterprises Limited, 225 Duncan Mill Road, Don Mills, Ontario, Canada M3B 3K9.

All characters in this book have no existence outside the imagination of the author and have no relation whatsoever to anyone bearing the same name or names. They are not even distantly inspired by any individual known or unknown to the author, and all incidents are pure invention.

This edition published by arrangement with Harlequin Books S.A.

® and TM are trademarks of the publisher. Trademarks indicated with ® are registered in the United States Patent and Trademark Office, the Canadian Trade Marks Office and in other countries.

www.eHarlequin.com

Printed in U.S.A.

ABOUT THE AUTHOR

After a career spent spinning words for clients ranging from corporate CEOs to talking fruits and vegetables, Kathleen Long now finds great joy spinning a world of fictional characters, places and plots. She shares her life with her husband, her daughter and their neurotic sheltie, dividing her time between suburban Philadelphia and the New Jersey seashore, where she can often be found—hands on keyboard, bare toes in sand—spinning tales. After all, life doesn't get much better than that. Please visit www.kathleenlong.com for the latest on contests, appearances and upcoming releases.

Books by Kathleen Long

Don't miss any of our special offers. Write to us at the following address for information on our newest releases.

Harlequin Reader Service
U.S.: 3010 Walden Ave., P.O. Box 1325, Buffalo, NY 14269
Canadian: P.O. Box 609, Fort Erie, Ont. L2A 5X3

CAST OF CHARACTERS

Wade Sorenson—When ecoterrorists target his latest construction project, he vows to fight back. But when the only witness is the son of the woman he's secretly loved for years, will he force the boy to testify, or protect the woman and her son, choosing love over justice?

Kerri Nelson—A widowed single mother, she'll do whatever it takes to protect her son. But will she be able to protect her heart from the man who vows to keep them both safe—and whom she holds responsible for her husband's death?

Thomas Weber—After being forbidden from playing near construction sites, he spots a lone figure running away from a local site just moments before a series of explosions and the death of an inspector. Now he's the sole witness to a violent crime, and someone is determined to keep him quiet.

Adam McCann—He's the local detective racing to keep his witness safe. He'll do whatever it takes to keep Thomas Weber unharmed, but are his intentions pure?

Michael Chase—Son of the local crime boss and a childhood friend of Wade Sorenson. When he becomes involved in the protection of Thomas Weber, he seems on the up-and-up, but can he really be trusted?

Vincent Chase—Head of a New Jersey crime organization, but also the man who helped Wade Sorenson get his start in construction. He doesn't want Wade anywhere near the family business, but just how far will he go to protect the man he considers a son?

John Weber—He died years before in an accident on one of Wade Sorenson's sites. Was it a tragic accident, or was he involved in something far more sinister than bricks and mortar?

Chapter One

Kerri Nelson never heard the glass she dropped shatter in the sink. As the series of explosions ripped through the quiet August afternoon, the dish towel slipped from her fingers, her heart catching in her chest.

Her mind raced through the possibilities—not of what had happened, but of where her son was. Where was Thomas? He'd taken his skateboard when he'd left an hour ago.

Where had he gone?

Fear danced along her spine, sending the small hairs at the back of her neck to attention.

Black smoke billowed into the crystal blue sky above the line of trees behind her home, and she sucked in a sharp breath. Close. Too close to home.

She hit the floor in an all-out sprint, slowing only long enough to yank open the kitchen door, focused on one thing only—Thomas.

As she raced through the woods and into the clearing,

flames licked at all but one of the six huge houses in the area's newest development. Pine Ridge Estates.

Anxiety pooled deep inside her. Tom had a fixation with construction sites, always had, ever since his daddy had taken him to work and gotten him his own tiny hard hat as a toddler.

She'd forbidden him from coming anywhere near this site. Had he defied her? Could he have been playing inside one of the partially constructed homes when something went horribly wrong?

Her gaze landed on a township truck parked at the edge of the dirt road, yet she saw no one. An inspector probably. She sent up a silent prayer that whoever had driven that truck onto the site was far from where the fires originated.

Sirens wailed in the distance, drawing nearer. Kerri's fear morphed into panic as she scanned the construction site and the surrounding woods for any sign of her son.

Her heart twisted in her chest.

"Thomas?" Her first attempt at calling her son's name was strangled, tight. "Thomas!" Her second wasn't much better.

"Mom."

The sound of his voice teased her through the smoke-filled air, but she couldn't locate the source. Couldn't see her son.

"Thomas!"

The blaring sirens were muffled beyond the pounding of her heart, the rush of her pulse in her ears. When her son emerged from behind a stand of trees, she saw him as if he were in slow motion, his face pale, but apparently without a scratch.

She ran as fast as her feet would carry her, gathering the nine-year-old who'd grown too old for hugs into her arms, hanging on for dear life. His arms locked around her waist and squeezed. When Kerri finally put enough space between them to tip his face to hers, she saw terror in his eyes.

"Are you hurt?"

He shook his head.

"Did you see what happened?"

Tom nodded. "Everything blew up. I'm sorry."

Sorry? Surely he didn't have a thing to do with what had happened.

A horn blared and Kerri realized the emergency vehicles were crossing Red Lion Road, getting ready to turn into the dirt path that gave access to the new community. She linked her arm through her son's and rushed him back toward the trees.

"Quickly," she said, fear palpable in her voice. "Did anyone see you here?"

"No," he answered, and relief surged through her.

They reached the cover of the woods just as a sea of vehicles and flashing lights careened onto the cul-de-sac, once lined with multimillion-dollar homes, now fringed by flames and smoke.

"Hurry." She urged Tom forward, away from the fire and destruction, back toward the safety of their home.

Sorenson Construction no doubt had insurance that would cover whatever accident had caused the explosion. Lord knew it wasn't the first accident on a Sorenson site.

Her stomach twisted and bile threatened to climb into her throat at the memory of another accident three years earlier. She shoved away the unwanted images—the hospital waiting room, the casket, friends and family gathered in her home.

Right now, Kerri needed to focus on her son's safety. Nothing else.

She locked the door behind them as they entered the kitchen, as if the brass bolt could keep them safe from whatever threat might lurk at the Sorenson site.

"I'm sorry." Tom dropped his gaze to the ceramic tile floor. "I wasn't supposed to go there."

"Ever." The sharpness of her tone startled Kerri and she read the surprise in her son's face as he lifted his focus to her.

"They put in new curbs," he said flatly. "Frankie said they were awesome for skateboarding."

Awesome for skateboarding.

Kerri closed her eyes and focused on her breathing. Her son was fine. He was unhurt. She needed to focus on that. But the reality was he could have been killed.

"I saw someone."

If possible, Tom's voice had grown even fainter and more frightened.

"From the township?" She snapped her eyes open and studied his expression. "The man from the truck?"

Tom nodded his head—slowly—as if he were afraid of what he'd seen. "I saw him, too. But he never came out again."

Never came out again.

My God.

"There was somebody else?" Countless thoughts battled for position inside Kerri's brain. Had the explosion been set on purpose? Had Tom witnessed a crime?

"He was running, Mom. The other man."

The little color that had been left in Tom's cheeks was gone now, making the blue of his eyes shocking next to his fair cheeks and sandy brown hair.

"Running where?" Kerri narrowed her gaze, her brain racing to keep up, to put the pieces of her son's story together.

"Away from the last house. Into the woods."

"From the fire?"

"Before the fire. Just before the fire. He came out of the last house after the inspector went into the first."

"Like he knew what was going to happen?"

Tom nodded, his gaze dropping back to the floor.

Fear squeezed at Kerri's throat, threatening to strangle her. What if the fire wasn't an accident, but something far more sinister? What if the man her son had seen had set the blaze? What if he'd seen her son?

She worked to steady her breathing, wanting to avoid panicking Tom any more than he already was.

"Did he see you?" She spoke the words slowly, distinctly, punctuating the importance of the question.

He shook his head.

"Are you sure?" Hope bubbled inside her.

Tom nodded and she pulled him into a hug, tucking his head protectively against her chest.

"Good," she whispered into his hair. "Let's keep this between you and me...deal?"

His head moved in another nod, and Kerri squeezed her eyes shut. Was she making a mistake? What if the inspector had been injured in the blast? What if Tom had seen something that might help the police figure out what had happened?

No. She mentally chastised herself. It was all too likely that the fire might be blamed on her son somehow, even though he'd had nothing to do with setting the blaze. After all, the investigation into the accident that had killed her husband had pointed the final finger of blame directly at the deceased.

She'd be damned if she'd let her son get anywhere near an investigation, especially an investigation involving Sorenson Construction.

As she held Tom close, she watched the fire's black smoke billow above the line of trees. She worked through her son's story in her head, repeating every word silently, analyzing every detail to see if she were making the right decision.

Awesome for skateboarding.

Tom hadn't had his skateboard when she'd found him at the site.

"Where's your skateboard, honey?"

He winced. "I dropped it when I ran."

Kerri swallowed. "Where?" Where investigators could find it? Where the man Tom had seen could find it?

She drew in a deep breath and held it, picturing the words she'd written on the bottom of the board with a permanent marker. Thomas Nelson. 122 Holly Drive.

She might as well have drawn a map.

She had to find that board before anyone else did.

Kerri pushed her son out to arm's length. "Where were you when you dropped it?"

He described a location not far from where she'd first seen him, and Kerri nodded her head, praying his memory hadn't been altered by shock or fear.

"Lock the door behind me and don't answer it for anyone."

Her son's pale eyes grew wide.

"I have to go find it. I don't want anyone to know you were there."

"Why?"

"Because," she answered, knowing her reply was unsatisfactory even for a nine-year-old. "Just because," she repeated.

A long while later, Kerri continued to pick her way through the foliage behind the houses, choking on the stench of burning lumber. The billowing smoke had shifted from black to white and she knew the operation would soon switch from fire fighting to investigation. She had to move quickly.

Relief surged through her when she spotted the wild

swirls of cobalt-blue and lime-green paint that covered the board. She knew her sense of urgency was partly irrational. If questioned, she could easily say Tom had lost the board on another day, at another time, but she wasn't taking chances.

Kerri had no sooner wrapped her fingers around the edge of the board and tucked it under one arm when she heard deep voices. Two unfamiliar, but one as familiar as a long lost friend.

Wade Sorenson.

The deep timbre reached into her heart and squeezed. Tears blurred her vision, but she blinked them back. She had no time to relive the pain she'd felt three years earlier, when Wade had betrayed her husband—his best friend.

She dropped into a squat and waited for the men to move farther away. The two strangers walked toward the one unburned home, and Wade turned back toward where a dark car had been parked.

Without looking back, Kerri took off in a sprint, praying she reached the deep cover of the pines before Wade spotted her.

Whatever mess Wade Sorenson had gotten himself into this time was no business of her son's. No business of hers. Sorenson could take care of himself.

All Kerri had to worry about was taking care of Thomas, and she wasn't going to let the man she'd once considered one of her closest friends inflict any more heartache on her family than he already had.

WADE STOOD BACK, arms crossed, and watched the tendrils of gray and white smoke wind their way up into the air. Emotions battled deep inside his gut. Anger. Disbelief. Denial.

The red lights of the emergency vehicles flashed like strobes, but the sirens had stopped now, the paramedics and police escort having left over twenty minutes earlier.

The township inspector had been in bad shape. Unconscious, burned and barely responsive. The poor guy had come to do a routine framing and electrical inspection, and instead he'd left fighting for his life.

Guilt spiraled in the pit of Wade's stomach. Had one of his guys installed the gas line incorrectly? Had a blowtorch been left on? What?

Pine Ridge Estates had been the culmination of a dream for him. He'd worked for years to build his company into one with a reputation home buyers would seek out. Sure, he'd almost lost it all after the Flamingo accident, but once the investigation had cleared him of any liability, he'd moved forward, rebuilding his reputation project by project. Until now.

Wood splintered and voices cried out as part of a framed ceiling gave way and crashed into the burned-out shell below. He winced, muttering a string of expletives.

Only one of the six houses remained untouched. Intact. The fire investigator, Charlie Forbes, emerged from the partially constructed building and walked toward where Wade stood. Wade moved to close the gap between them, anxious to hear the man's take on what had happened.

Was it possible the township inspector had done something to cause the series of explosions? Wade drew in a deep breath, then sighed. Not likely. What had happened here today was no accident. He'd been targeted. Wade knew it in his gut, as much as he wanted to deny it.

Once they were within earshot of each other, Forbes spoke. "The sixth incendiary device didn't blow."

Incendiary device. Sonofa—

"Signature's consistent with Project Liberation," the investigator continued. "I've called in the Feds."

Project Liberation.

Ecoterrorism.

Wade's stomach did a slow sideways pitch. He'd known developing this community on the fringe of the South Jersey Pinelands might affront certain ecologically minded types, but he'd gone through the proper channels, including community meetings and hearings. His plan had been approved with flying colors, to the liking of everyone he'd met.

Obviously, not to the liking of the powers within the Project Liberation organization.

"Are you sure?" he asked.

The investigator nodded, then gestured for Wade to follow him. They made their way around the houses until they stood close to where the third shell smoldered.

Forbes pointed at a portion of the home's back wall.

Two words had been spray painted in black. *No Sprawl.*

"I've read about this." Wade uttered the words on the heels of a frustrated breath. "I didn't know they'd developed an interest in the Pine Barrens."

"Apparently, they have," Forbes answered.

"Can I go inside?" Wade jerked a thumb toward the only unscathed home.

Forbes shook his head. "Can't do that. We need to keep the specifics quiet. Chain of evidence. That sort of thing."

Wade frowned. "Surely you don't think I had anything to do with this?"

The other man shrugged. "Don't take this personally, but one of the first things we look at is possible insurance fraud."

Wade pointed to the spray-painted graffiti. "Even with this?"

"Anyone can buy a can of spray paint."

Forbes's attention was pulled away as a dark sedan eased to a stop behind a ladder truck, its tires sinking into the now thick mud. "Task force is here," he said as he walked away from Wade, making it clear their discussion was over.

"Wade. Long time no see." The driver of the car raised his hand in greeting. "Forbes."

"McCann." Wade and Forbes spoke simultaneously.

Detective Adam McCann was one of Wade's oldest friends. He was also the newly appointed head of the county task force on Homeland Security.

"What have we got?" McCann asked as he stopped

next to Wade, momentarily clasping a hand on his shoulder. "You doing all right?"

Wade nodded and Forbes jerked a thumb toward the smoldering houses behind them. "Clean evidence in the sixth house. Matches the devices in the other five."

"Liberation?" McCann asked.

"Signature's there." Forbes nodded.

"Any word on the inspector?" Wade asked.

McCann pursed his lips and gave a quick shake of his head. "Not yet. I called in on the way over here. Doesn't look good, though."

"Damn." Wade dropped his gaze to the ground.

"We'll get them." McCann stepped toward one of the burned-out shells. "Let's take a look before the Feds get here and screw everything up."

"Follow me," Forbes answered. He stopped in his tracks when Wade moved to follow. "This won't take long."

Wade stood silently as he watched the two disappear into the skeleton of a five-thousand-square-foot estate home. He moved toward McCann's car and rested one hip on the fender.

Project Liberation.

Chances were if he rebuilt, they'd strike again. But maybe McCann and his task force could take them down. He didn't know much about the ecoterrorism group, but he knew they were very careful, and very clean. They left their signature, but nothing else. Nothing that would point to any one individual.

Their organization prided itself on the lack of any sort of paper trail. One suspected bomber had been arrested out in Montana, but Wade couldn't remember hearing anything else.

A sudden movement in the woods beyond the homes captured his attention, sending all thoughts of Project Liberation far from his mind.

The flash of long, auburn hair was unmistakable. Even after all these years, he knew the owner's identity immediately. He'd been admiring that particular head of hair since high school.

Kerri Nelson.

She and her son lived just on the other side of the dense foliage. But why would she show up at the crime scene? Morbid curiosity? Not her style.

Even more importantly, why had she run? The familiar old guilt twisted at his insides. She'd obviously seen him and wanted to get as far away as she could, as quickly as possible.

Adam McCann emerged from the house alone, and Wade pulled his focus out of the past and into the present.

"Hop in. We'll talk," Adam said as he pulled open the car's front door.

When they'd both settled into their seats, Adam handed an unopened cup of coffee to Wade, then took a sip from a second one.

"Anything you want to tell me?"

Wade shot his friend a sharp glare. "I had nothing to do with this."

"Good," McCann answered. "I still have to question you."

"When?" Wade drew in a deep breath and took a hit of the bitter coffee.

"Later's good. Now's better."

"I can follow you to the station." Wade met his friend's visual scrutiny head-on. "I've got nothing to hide."

"Hell of a thing." McCann turned his gaze back to the smoldering rubble. "Insured?"

"Always," Wade answered.

"We're not going to get anywhere without a witness, you know that, right?" The skin between McCann's eyes puckered into a crease. "These people are like ghosts. Just about impossible to catch."

Wade nodded, disappointment balling inside him. "I figured as much. What about the inspector?"

"It'll be a miracle if he recovers, but right now he's our only hope. The scene is clean. They knew what they were doing."

He put down his coffee and pinned Wade with a glare. "No one else scheduled to be out here today?"

Wade shook his head. "We were waiting on the inspection."

"Well—" McCann pulled in a sharp breath "—we'll question surrounding residents. Make sure no one was out here at the time of the blast. I'll get that started while you and I head downtown."

The image of Kerri's retreating back flashed through Wade's mind. Should he tell McCann she'd been at the scene? After all, how long could she have been there? Certainly not long enough to be responsible in any way. The investigator had walked the entire scene and the surrounding woods. If Forbes had seen her, they would have heard about it.

Wade reached for the door handle, suddenly needing to get out of the cramped space. "I'll be right behind you."

"See if you can come up with a list of anyone who might hold a grudge against you."

McCann's words stopped Wade cold. He hesitated, half-in and half-out of the car.

"I thought the signature was consistent with Project Liberation?"

McCann nodded, narrowing his gaze. "True. But they've hit enough targets for their signature to be known. Can't rule out a copycat."

He twisted on the ignition, and Wade pushed himself out of the car.

"See you in a few," McCann called out just as Wade slammed the door.

Wade slapped his palm against the glass and stepped clear of the car's tires as McCann pulled away.

Anyone who might hold a grudge against you.

McCann's words echoed in his brain as he headed for his truck.

There was one person who definitely held a grudge, but she wasn't capable of something like this. Yet she had been at the scene. Wade had no idea how long, or why, but she'd been here.

Kerri had made it very clear after John's funeral that she wanted nothing to do with Wade ever again. He'd respected her wishes. Until now.

Now an innocent man had been critically injured and Pine Ridge Estates had suffered millions of dollars worth of damage. Wade had every intention of finding out exactly why he'd been targeted and by whom.

Even though he knew McCann and his team would leave no stone unturned, he had to talk to Kerri. Maybe she'd seen something—seen someone. Then again, maybe she hadn't. No matter. If she knew anything at all, Wade had to know.

He and Kerri Nelson were about to have their first reunion after three long years.

Whether she wanted to, or not.

Chapter Two

Kerri sipped on her hot tea and glanced out the window. The heavy rumble of fire trucks had ceased and the late afternoon sun had begun to slip behind the trees, casting long shadows across the sandy yard out front.

A pair of detectives had come and gone, wanting to know if she'd seen or heard anything over at Pine Ridge. She'd lied to their faces and maintained a calm composure. Matter of fact, the ease of lying had surprised her.

She'd never thought herself capable, at least not to two police officers, yet she'd had no problem telling them that yes, she'd heard the explosions and sirens, but that no, she hadn't seen a thing. She'd gone on to explain her son had been in his bedroom all day, terribly ill with chicken pox.

She was no fool. Neither of the officers so much as asked to speak with Tom, taking her word as gospel and probably wanting to avoid the boy's alleged germs more than they wanted to question him.

The deception had been easy, and when the whisper

of guilt flared inside her, she batted it away. Nothing she or Tom had seen would make a difference.

Except the man who ran away, her conscience whispered.

She frowned as a hunter green pickup pulled into the drive, easing down the private lane and coming to a stop next to her SUV. When the driver emerged from behind the tinted glass her breath caught. She lowered her cup to the windowsill, afraid she might spill its contents.

"Tommy," she called out to her son, now happily glued to a television video game. "I need you to run back upstairs for a bit."

"Aw, Mom."

Normally, her son's whine would have set her teeth on edge, but her only concern now was keeping him as far from Wade as possible.

She stepped away from the window just as Wade began his walk across her slate stepping stones, leisurely making his way past her carefully manicured flower beds.

Kerri hurried into the center hall, crossed to the television and pushed off the power button. Tom's eyes grew huge, then morphed into narrowed slits.

She jerked her thumb toward the stairs. "Quickly," she whispered, just as Wade's knock sounded at the front door.

She waited until Tommy had cleared the top step before she put her hand on the doorknob, drawing in a deep, steadying breath.

"Who is it?"

"You know perfectly well who it is," Wade answered. "I saw you looking out the window."

Damn the man.

Kerri jerked the door open, three years worth of pent-up anger boiling inside her. "You're not welcome here."

Wade's dark eyebrows lifted, but his stare never left her face. She fought the urge to shift her weight from one foot to the other, an effect he'd had on her since the day they'd first met.

The tanned skin around his eyes held more creases than she remembered, and his rich, brown hair showed the slightest glimmer of gray at his temples. The subtle signs of age had made him more handsome than ever.

She shook off the thought and reminded herself of his role in John's death. The memory effectively smothered any lingering fondness she felt for the man.

"What?" she asked, hoping her sharp tone would leave no doubt he wasn't getting across the threshold.

As if reading her mind, he lifted one workboot to the sill. Kerri dropped her focus to his foot, then narrowed the opening of the door.

When she returned her attention to his face, his expression had shifted from warm to intense.

"Did you hear about the fire?"

"Hard not to," she answered. "I've already spoken to the police. I've got nothing to say to you."

"I saw you." The dark eyebrows lifted again, and the line of his jaw grew sharp.

Kerri blinked, but fought to keep any additional reaction out of her features. "I'm not sure what you're talking about."

Wade nodded. "You saw me and you ran, didn't you?"

She made a snapping noise with her mouth and shook her head, unable to force a suitable response out of her brain.

"In the woods." Wade leaned so close his warm breath brushed her face. "Behind the houses. I saw you run away."

"Uncle Wade?"

Tom's voice cut through their standoff, and Kerri stiffened. "Damn," she muttered under her breath.

Footsteps pounded down the staircase, and Tom squeezed between her and the door frame, launching himself at Wade.

The man pulled her son into an embrace, all signs of confrontation disappearing from his face as he beamed at the child.

"Who's this?" He ruffled her son's hair. "And what did you do with that little squirt who used to beat me in basketball?"

Tom laughed, and Kerri caught herself smiling. Her son's laughter had become a rare commodity since his father's death. The sound never failed to bring a smile to her lips, even if the cause was Wade Sorenson.

"You might as well come in," she said, pulling the door open wide.

Wade released Tom and followed the boy inside.

"You look good, Red," he whispered in Kerri's ear as he brushed past her shoulder.

Kerri shot him a glare as she closed the door. If the man thought the use of her old nickname would warm her feelings toward him, he had another thing coming.

It would be a cold day in hell before she willingly welcomed Wade Sorenson back into either her heart or her home.

WADE HAD NEVER SEEN such fury in the blue depths of Kerri's eyes. Not even in the days following John's death. Back then, her eyes had been full of pain and grief.

He hadn't seen her since they'd buried John—and their friendship—but it was apparent the years had replaced her grief with a hard-edged anger.

There'd been a time once—many years earlier—when Wade thought what he felt for Kerri went far deeper than friendship, but his best friend had beat him to the punch, asking out the fiery redhead before Wade could muster the courage to do the same.

He'd watched John and Kerri fall in love, marry, give birth to Tom. He'd watched them struggle through marital difficulties, financial stress and parenting. And he'd watched Kerri bury her husband, watched Tom say goodbye to his father.

Wade drew in a deep breath and held it, bolstering his resolve. He might not have been prepared for the magnitude of the anger in Kerri's once warm blue eyes, but he could handle it.

He intended to get to the bottom of what had happened today, and if he had to use Kerri and Tom to gain that information, so be it.

Tom slid into a chair at the kitchen table and Wade mirrored his movement. Without asking, Kerri poured them each a glass of milk then placed a sleeve of cookies in the middle of the table.

The familiar action enveloped Wade in a wave of memories, and for the briefest of moments, the past three years slid away, carrying him to the happy time before the accident. Before John's death.

The reason for his visit brought him crashing back to the present.

"So have you seen my new site?" he asked Tom.

Kerri shot him an angry glare as she dropped into the chair directly across from him.

Tom nodded. "It's great for skateboarding."

Wade hesitated for a moment. The new curbs hadn't gone in until earlier this week. If Tom had tried them out, he'd been to the site recently.

"So he's heard." Kerri spoke before Wade had a chance to ask Tom the obvious question. "He's forbidden from going to the site," she continued. "We're well aware of how dangerous construction sites can be."

Wade winced, then felt like hell as Tommy dropped his chin, lowering his gaze to his lap.

"So, you've never been there?" He directed the question at Tom, willing Kerri to keep her mouth shut.

"I just told—"

"I'm asking Tom," he interrupted her, his tone growing sharp. Too sharp.

Kerri scraped her chair back against the hardwood kitchen floor. "I think you'd better go."

"You know a man was critically injured there today, Tom. If you saw anything at all, you should tell the police."

He watched as the boy frowned, feeling like a bully for pressuring the kid, but growing desperate to get the admission he thought Tom might be withholding.

Suddenly, Tom lifted his gaze to Wade's, his blue eyes far too serious for someone so young.

"The guy in the truck?"

"Tommy," Kerri admonished.

Wade nodded. "Yeah, the guy in the truck. Did you see anybody else?"

Tom looked nervously from Wade to his mother and back.

"He's not getting involved, Wade." Kerri's voice shook with emotion. "I won't let him."

Wade pushed back, standing toe to toe with Kerri. He gripped her elbows, holding her near. "If he saw something, he's our only witness, Kerri. No one else was there. We can stop whoever did this."

She visibly softened, and Wade thought she was a breath away from agreeing, when the emotional shutters returned to her stubborn gaze.

"No," she said flatly. "You're on your own."

Disappointment and anger battled inside him. "If

you're afraid of retaliation, no one but the investigators on the case need to know. We'll keep it out of the media."

Fear shimmered in Kerri's eyes. So he'd hit the nail on the head.

"Haven't you brought us enough heartache?" She pulled free of his grip and moved toward her son. "Tom, honey, tell your Uncle Wade goodbye. You need to get cleaned up for dinner."

Disappointment flashed in Tom's eyes, but he did as he was told. After he'd moved out of earshot, Kerri spoke again.

"Your insurance will cover your loss, right? Leave my son out of this."

"Is this what you want to teach him, Red? You want to teach him not to cooperate instead of trying to make a difference."

Color flared in her cheeks. "Don't ever call me that again."

She might as well have slapped him.

Without another word, Kerri moved from the kitchen to the hallway to the front door, jerking the heavy wooden door open.

"We never had this conversation. If you care at all about Thomas and me, you'll walk out of this door and you won't come back."

"Why did you go to the site? You know what he saw, don't you?"

"He didn't see anything, Wade. He dropped his skateboard and ran when the fires started. I went back for his board." She slowly shook her head from side to side. "That's all. You need to leave us alone."

There was no denying the fury in Kerri's voice, but Wade spotted more than anger in her eyes. He'd known the woman long enough to know she was bluffing.

"You're lying."

She bristled, but stepped nearer, so near Wade could pick up the soft scent of her soap.

"I will not let you drag my son into this. Is that understood? He saw nothing."

"I don't believe you." He hesitated, searching for the right words. "I'd never let anything happen to him. Why won't you trust me?"

One of her auburn eyebrows lifted, as if she couldn't believe he'd asked the question. "Get out of my house."

"The police think Project Liberation did this, but they need a witness."

"Leave."

Wade stepped out onto the front step, tensing as the door slammed behind him. He'd give her this round, but if she thought she'd won the battle, Kerri Nelson was in for a rude awakening.

IS THIS WHAT you want to teach him?

Wade's words echoed through Kerri's brain as she cracked open the top of her jewelry box later that night. The polished amethyst heart lay safely beneath the box's velvet tray, still tucked into its pink drawstring bag, even after all of this time.

There had been moments over the years when she'd wondered if she'd married the right friend. Her school-girl crush had been on Wade, yet it had been John who had pursued her and married her.

Wade had never fought for her, never expressed an interest in her. She traced a finger across the smooth, cool stone. Except for this. He'd given her this on Valentine's Day, just hours before John had asked her out for the first time.

She returned the stone to its bag, drew the satin ribbon tight and dropped it into the jewelry box, replacing the tray and closing the lid shut with a snap.

It didn't matter now whether or not she had once cared for Wade. John had given her a son she loved more than life itself, a son so much like his father, her breath sometimes caught at the mere sight of his crooked smile.

She'd trusted Wade Sorenson years ago, and then he'd let her down, betraying her trust and her friendship.

Now he wanted her to trust him again—with Tom's safety.

As Kerri clicked off her bedroom light and stared out the window into the Pinelands, she wasn't sure if she'd ever be able to trust Wade again. But one thing was certain.

She'd do whatever it took to protect her son. No matter the cost.

Hours later, after a sleepless night, she groaned at Tom's words at breakfast.

"I want to help, Mom."

Kerri looked up from the skillet and glared at her son. "No."

"But Uncle Wade said I'm the only witness."

And once the police knew that, chances were whoever set the explosions would know that, too. Kerri wasn't naive enough to think the local law enforcement officers could keep that news quiet.

"They can do this without you, trust me."

Defeat overtook the determined expression on her son's face, and for a moment, Kerri thought about cooperating with the police. Was she wrong to encourage her son not to care? Not to help?

According to Wade Sorenson she was, but Wade had his own agenda, didn't he? After all, his reputation had taken a hit after her husband's accident. Surely this incident—domestic terrorism or not—wouldn't do a thing to help that reputation along. The quicker they got the investigation resolved, the better it would be for Wade.

Well, she wasn't worried about Wade. She was worried about Tom. Anyone who was capable of the crime her son had witnessed, was no doubt capable of far worse if it meant keeping the lone witness quiet.

When the phone rang, she answered without waiting for the caller ID readout. Her stomach tightened at the sound of Wade's voice.

"How'd you sleep?"

"Like a baby," she lied. "You?"

"Not a wink."

Silence stretched across the line, and Kerri held her tongue.

"Have you made your decision?" he asked.

"I thought I made myself perfectly clear last night."

She waited for his response as a fresh silence beat between them.

"The township inspector died this morning."

Kerri's breath caught, and she leaned against the kitchen counter.

"We're talking about murder now." Wade spoke with an intensity she'd never before heard in his voice. "Murder, Kerri. In your backyard."

"On your construction site," she shot back.

"He left three kids."

Wade's words sucked the air from her lungs, sending her memory racing back to the moment she'd found out John was dead. She would never wish that horrific reality on another wife, on another child.

"Don't they deserve to find out who did this?" Wade asked softly.

"Yes." Kerri's voice was barely more than a whisper.

"What?"

"Yes," she repeated. "You heard me. What guarantee do I have that Tom's identity will be protected?"

At the breakfast table, Tom straightened, excitement shimmering in his eyes. He was too young to know there was a huge difference between what he read in his detective novels and real life.

"You have my word," Wade said.

Kerri resisted the urge to tell him his word was worthless in her book. Tom didn't need to hear that. The kid still worshipped Wade like the hero they all once thought he was.

"The police can come to us," she said.

"Can't do it. You've got to come in. I'll pick you up and we can use the back entrance."

"I can drive myself, thanks. Just tell me where to go." She glanced at the hand-painted clock on the wall over the sink. "We'll be there in an hour."

The sooner they got this over with, the better. Once Tom made his ID—or not—they could return to life as normal, and Wade Sorenson could fade back into their past, where he belonged.

Chapter Three

Wade stood quietly, observing the police sketch artist as he guided Tom through the process of developing a likeness of the man he'd seen. The boy's review of suspected Project Liberation member photos had gotten them nowhere. Tom hadn't recognized a single face as that of the man at Pine Ridge.

Kerri sat at McCann's desk, nervously watching her son. Wade couldn't help but notice the dark smudges beneath her eyes, nor the lines of worry across her forehead.

So much for her story about sleeping like a baby. She looked like she'd been up all night. He couldn't blame her for the way she'd acted when he'd been at the house, for not wanting Tom to cooperate. After all, the boy was all she had left. She was smart enough to know Project Liberation was a dangerous organization.

He moved to rest a hand on her slender shoulder, but she leaned away from his touch. There had been a time when she would have leaned on Wade for support, when she *had* leaned on Wade for support. All that changed when Wade's own testimony during the investigation into John's death had directed the blame at her husband.

Maybe he should have lied to protect his friend's memory. Maybe he should have let his company take the blame, but he hadn't. He'd chosen the truth instead.

The doubt whispering through him was nothing new.

Wade blew out a frustrated breath and moved away from where Kerri sat, not wanting to cause her any additional discomfort. McCann caught his eye and gave him the thumbs-up. Wade stole a glance at the sketch and realized the artist was almost done. The suspect's hair, nose and mouth—every feature—had been captured in crystal clear detail.

Tom had done an incredible job of providing the necessary descriptions.

When the sketch artist gave McCann the signal that they were through, the detective gathered Tom and Kerri and walked them briskly out of the room. Tom shot a quick glance at Wade, who winked in return, but Kerri never so much as looked his way, keeping her eyes averted as if the sight of him might turn her to stone.

He sank into the battered chair next to McCann's desk and waited for his friend's return. He didn't have to sit still for long. McCann returned almost immediately, and Wade realized he must have handed off the Nelsons to someone else.

"What do you think?" he asked as McCann slipped back into his chair.

"We'll get it out there." McCann gripped the sketch tightly in one hand. "If this guy's local, we'll get him."

"I promised the mother the kid's name wouldn't leak out."

McCann nodded. "I heard you the first three times you told me. You have my word on it."

Wade tipped his head toward a small gathering of detectives on the far side of the room. "What about their word?"

McCann scowled. "They're pros, Wade. They aren't going to broadcast the identity of our only witness. Relax."

But as Wade stood amidst the ruins of Pine Ridge Estates a short while later, he couldn't help but worry. Whoever had coordinated this devastation had also been a pro. A pro with an agenda.

How much of a risk did Tom present as a witness? The kid had obviously had a clear view of the bomber's face. Wade could only hope the suspect hadn't had a clear view in return.

If word of a witness got out, just how far would the bomber—hell, Project Liberation—go to keep him quiet?

The ecoterrorists prided themselves on destroying only property, not lives. But now that they'd crossed that line, now that the inspector had died, what were they capable of doing to avoid paying the penalty for murder? To avoid getting caught?

The stench of the fire hung heavy in the summer heat, and Wade silently cursed himself. Maybe he'd been wrong to involve Tom and Kerri. Maybe he should have left the investigation up to McCann and his team.

He turned away from the burned-out shells of the luxury homes, back toward his dust-covered pickup.

Kerri was wrong about being the only one responsible for Tom. Wade was responsible now, too. He might have failed John's memory in life, but he planned to honor that memory now.

By protecting his wife and son.

KERRI BRUSHED a lock of hair from Tom's forehead as he slept, pride welling inside her. He'd been such a little man today. Brave and confident.

He'd had one heck of a day, and the excitement had caught up to him. He'd practically fallen asleep at the dinner table, his head bobbing dangerously close to his bowl of chili.

She'd been amazed when he didn't protest her suggestion that he get ready for bed early. She'd been even more surprised when he'd asked for his Uncle Wade as she'd tucked the covers around his shoulders.

Kerri knew Tom was hungry for male influence in his life, knew he missed his father terribly, but inviting Wade back into their lives would be a mistake.

She'd sat next to Tom's bed until his breathing had grown even and steady, his features relaxing into peaceful sleep.

Kerri flashed back on the feel of Wade's hand on her shoulder earlier at the police station. His brief touch had ignited an angry tangle of fury and need inside her. There were times she wanted someone to lean on, wanted someone to help her navigate life without John, but allowing Wade to be that person wasn't an option.

He'd made his choice, and now they all had to live with the consequences.

When the phone rang, she rushed to pick up the receiver, wanting to stop the ringing before the noise woke her son.

"Hello," she spoke into the phone.

The only sound that greeted her was silence. She glanced at the caller ID readout. Blank.

She hadn't given the machine enough time to register the number, and she pressed the phone back to her ear.

"Is anyone there?"

The silence grew deafening, and just as she was about to hang up, the caller drew in a deep, rattling breath.

"You should have minded your own business." The voice was deep and gruff, and chilled her to the bone. The voice was obviously male, but not that of anyone she knew.

"Who is this?" Kerri was barely able to push the words through the trepidation squeezing at her throat.

"Don't talk to the cops again."

The line clicked dead, and she froze momentarily, the receiver still pressed to her ear, her heart pounding in her chest.

She dropped the phone and raced back to Tom's room, releasing a relieved breath when she spotted his sleeping form, unmoved from where she'd left him. Safe. Unharmed.

Returning to her own room, anger began to press through her fear, and she snatched the phone from the floor, dialing Wade's number from memory.

He'd promised her—promised Tom—he'd keep their identities a secret.

He'd lied. Again.

He picked up the phone on the third ring.

"How could you do it?" Kerri heard the hysteria in her own voice and worked to calm herself before she spoke again.

"Red?" Wade sounded groggy, as if the turmoil and emotion of the past two days had caught up to him, just as it had caught up to Tom.

"They know, Wade. They know."

"Who knows? What happened?" His voice was sharp now, alert and focused.

"I got a call. He told me not to talk to the cops again." Tears shimmered in her vision as she spoke, and she blinked them away, willing herself to hold it together. "He said we should have minded our own business."

"I'm calling McCann."

"No." Kerri's voice boomed. "No more. Tom's done helping you." A tear slid down her face and she sniffed as she swiped it away.

"I'm coming over. Don't answer the phone or let anyone else in until I get there."

Before she could protest, Wade was gone. She took

the phone with her into Tom's room where she sat, in the dark, watching her son sleep, silently vowing to keep the voice on the phone as far away from him as possible.

WADE DROVE LIKE a bat out of hell, sliding his pickup into the mouth of Kerri's driveway. His pulse had pounded in his ears ever since she'd told him about her mystery caller.

Damn. How had word leaked out about Tom's involvement? Was McCann to blame? One of his men? Had someone from the media been lurking outside the station? Or did Project Liberation have someone on the inside?

He shoved the truck into Park, cut the ignition and launched himself from the driver's seat, covering the ground between the truck and the house in several long strides.

Kerri yanked the door open just as he raised his hand to knock.

"I heard you pull up." Moisture glistened in her eyes, mixed with the anger that had taken up permanent residence there. She still gripped the phone in her hand, and Wade reached for it, prying the receiver out of her tense fingers.

"Where's Tom?" He pressed a hand to her back, and when she didn't move away, a measure of relief eased through him.

"Sleeping."

He led Kerri into the kitchen and pulled out a chair.

She lowered herself into the seat then dropped her face to her palms.

"I'm sorry. I never thought this would happen." He squatted next to her, putting one hand on her knee.

This time, she shoved him away, raising her gaze to meet his. "You didn't think." She scowled at him. "You didn't think at all."

"McCann gave me his word—"

"Apparently his word is worth just about as much as yours is." Kerri cut him off before he could finish his thought.

Wade opened his mouth to protest, but hesitated. "You're right," he said, instead.

The surprise that flickered through her features was unmistakable.

"I should have thought this through. I should have left you and Tom out of this. You've been through enough." He cupped her chin in his hand. "I'm sorry."

Kerri blinked, visibly softening for a moment before she pushed away from him, standing, then crossing to the kitchen window.

"Right now, I don't care whether you're sorry or not." She spoke softly, intently. "I care about you keeping us safe. That's one promise you'd better keep."

"I'll call McCann in the morning. Find out who's behind the leak."

"The caller said no more cops."

"We can trust McCann. And I trust him not to tell another soul about your caller."

She studied him intently, then nodded, the movement so slight it was barely detectable. "I'm going upstairs. I want to be with Tom."

"I'll sleep on the sofa." Wade reached for her as she passed, lightly gripping her elbow.

Kerri hesitated, meeting his look with eyes that had morphed from determined to exhausted. "There's a blanket in the family room closet."

"I remember."

She nodded, then walked out of the kitchen. Wade waited until she'd climbed the steps, waited until he heard Tom's bedroom door open and then close again before he moved an inch. He plucked the coffeepot from its stand and filled the water reservoir for ten cups.

He had no intention of sleeping on the sofa or anywhere else tonight.

As long as Kerri and Tom were asleep upstairs, he'd be awake downstairs. Standing guard.

WADE STOOD AT the front door and watched Tom head off on his bike to deliver papers. He smiled as the kid bounced his bike over the gravel drive, oblivious to the fact that somewhere out there, someone was furious there'd been a witness to the Pine Ridge fires.

"Are you sure this is such a good idea?" Kerri's tired voice sounded close behind him. He turned to watch her drying a breakfast plate, going through the motion like a robot. An exhausted robot.

"Why don't you try to get some sleep?" He reached

for the plate and towel, taking them from her and tipping his chin toward the staircase.

"It's okay." She shook her head and frowned. "I slept a little."

"I'm not buying that one again." Wade returned his focus to the drive, catching just a glimpse of Tom as he vanished out into the street.

"You didn't sleep, either." Kerri stepped next to him, looking past him out into the yard. "Sofa wasn't touched and if I'm not mistaken, half my can of coffee has gone missing."

He stole a glimpse at her profile, detecting just the slightest hint of a smile at the corner of her lips. "Must have been Tom."

"Right." She looked at him, her features hinting at the warmth he'd missed for the past three years. "Thanks for watching out for us."

With that, she took the plate and towel away from him and headed back to the kitchen.

Thanks for watching out for us.

Wade thought of Thomas—alone—out on the quiet road, delivering papers along the route he'd no doubt followed countless times before.

A habit.

A routine.

Dread coiled into a tight knot in Wade's gut, and he reached into his pocket, wrapping his fingers around the keys to his truck.

What if whoever had made the call last night knew

more about the Nelsons than just their phone number? What if he knew where they lived? Where Tom went to school? What time he set out every morning on his paper route?

"I'll be right back," he called out as he pushed out into the warm August morning and trotted across the stepping stones toward his truck.

His imagination might be in overdrive, but suddenly Wade couldn't imagine why he'd ever let Tom head out the front door alone in the first place.

HE WAITED FOR the boy to round the corner, emerging from the private lane, headed toward the housing community a half mile down the road.

The description fit. Correct size. Correct approximate age. Correct hair color.

He kept his foot pressed on the van's brake until the boy was far enough ahead that following at a distance wouldn't draw unnecessary attention.

The boy's paper-delivery bag bounced against his back as he careened over the gravel shoulder and onto the asphalt road. He then steered the bike back onto the shoulder, then back onto the asphalt, repeating the move like a game. Bouncing the front tire as he did so, holding his body up off the seat, as if riding a wave.

It was a shame the kid had to be silenced, but an order was an order. The driver shook his head. He had no choice. Keeping the kid quiet was the only way they could carry out the rest of the plan.

The pieces had begun to fall into place, and they couldn't afford to be derailed now—by a witness— even if that witness was just a kid. The game had changed once the local inspector had died.

Careless.

He'd been careless. The construction site had been clear when he'd set the devices. He hadn't even spotted the inspector's truck when he'd fled the scene, only hearing about the victim later on, from news reports.

Silencing the kid would redeem his mistake and keep the organization intact.

He pressed down on the accelerator, closing the gap between the van and the bike. The plan was a simple one.

A hit-and-run.

A fatal accident wouldn't be a first for this isolated stretch of road, but it would be the last for the witness.

Just a few more yards and the threat of exposure would be eliminated.

Permanently.

Chapter Four

Wade pulled to the end of the drive, quickly glanced to make sure the road was clear, then turned in the direction Tom had taken. He pressed the accelerator to the floor and squinted down the road, frowning when he realized a plain white van obscured his view.

A plain white van.

Suspicion rolled through him, and as much as he tried to tell himself his imagination was working overtime, he couldn't convince himself otherwise.

The phone call to Kerri had been real, just as any perceived threat to Tom had to be considered real.

The van's brake lights illuminated briefly, the vehicle slowing just enough for Wade to make out Tom's figure not far in front of the truck. The kid was so busy bouncing his bike on and off the edge of the road he was no doubt oblivious to the fact there was a van close behind him.

The van accelerated suddenly. Wade's heart stopped cold in his chest. What in the hell was the driver doing?

And then he realized.

The driver was aiming for Tom.

Wade hit his horn, keeping one palm pressed to the steering wheel to keep the sound blaring as he floored the truck, urging it forward. As he closed the distance between him and the van, he searched for any sign of a license plate, but saw none.

None.

A plain white van without a license plate on a deserted stretch of road steering straight for the sole witness to a violent crime.

He needed no imagination to put those pieces together.

Wade pounded the horn now, a quick series of loud blares, hoping he'd jolt Tom from his play and alert him to the danger closing in from behind.

Just as Wade's truck closed to within inches of the van's bumper, the vehicle swerved sharply toward the shoulder, its right wheels dipping into the sandy soil. The brake lights never illuminated; if anything, the van sped up.

Tom.

My God.

Fear seized Wade's heart and twisted.

Just as quickly as the van had swerved off the road, it swerved back on and sped away. Wade braked, frantically searching for any sign of Tom or his bike.

Then he spotted it. A chrome wheel rim, spinning upside down between a small stand of firs.

"Tom," he uttered the word on the breath of a

whisper, skidding his truck to a stop, slamming it into Park and launching himself out of the driver's seat.

Kerri would never forgive him. Hell, he'd never forgive himself. Why had he been so intent on bringing whoever had torched Pine Ridge to justice?

Was erasing any doubt about his own reputation or insurance fraud so important he'd risk Tom's safety?

"Tom!"

He raced toward the spot where the bike wheel spun, slowing as it lost momentum. Something in the foliage moved and Tom's pale face appeared from behind the trees. "What happened?"

Wade reached him in two strides and pulled him into an embrace. "Did the van hit you?"

"No." Tom shook his head slightly. "I heard the beeping and I figured he was out of control or something. I ditched into the trees and got out of the way."

"Good job, buddy." Wade shot up a silent prayer of thanks and breathed the words into Tom's hair. "Good job."

Tom pushed away from Wade and turned toward his bike. "Think it's ruined?"

Wade shook his head, reaching to pull the bike from the trees, wanting only to get Tom back to the safety of Kerri's house. "We'll fix it. Don't worry." He tipped his chin toward the truck. "Climb in. Let's get you home."

"But my papers."

"Throw them in the back. We'll figure something out."

As Tom settled into the passenger seat next to Wade, the boy frowned. "Do you think that guy will be all right? Maybe his brakes are out or something."

"Or something," Wade muttered. "Let's just say I think he'll get what's coming to him."

Tom's gaze narrowed, but Wade said nothing more as he made a three-point turn and headed back toward Kerri's drive, silently vowing to make sure the driver got exactly what was coming to him.

KERRI HAD JUST RETURNED the last of the breakfast dishes to the kitchen cabinet when Tom's voice rang out from the front of the house.

"Mom!"

The anxiousness palpable in his one word sent her heart lurching into her throat. She spun away from the kitchen counter just as her son cleared the doorway and launched himself into her arms. He buried his head against her denim shirt and she wrapped her arms around him, holding tight, not asking the questions pounding through her brain.

What happened?

Are you all right?

What are you doing back from your route so early?

When Wade stepped into the kitchen, his face ashen, their eyes met and held. In that moment, Kerri knew all she needed to know. Something had gone wrong. Horribly wrong.

Had someone tried to hurt her son—or worse? Had

it been whoever called last night? Was it the man who'd set the devices at the Pine Ridge site?

The details didn't matter.

Her son's safety did.

"I'm sorry." Wade spoke the words flatly, in a defeated tone.

Tom pushed away from Kerri's embrace, his eyes bright with a mix of excitement and fear. "You should have seen it, Mom. This guy in a van, he was out of control. I ditched into the trees and then Wade was there. I think the guy's brakes were out or something."

Or something, Kerri thought.

Wade winced when she glared at him and she knew she'd hit the mark.

Her son's close call hadn't been an accident.

Whoever wanted Tom's silence apparently wasn't going to sit around and give the boy a second chance. Well, she had no intention of giving Tom's attacker a second chance at her son.

She squeezed Tom's upper arms. "Run up to your room for a minute, honey."

"But my route…"

Genuine concern shone brightly in his eyes and she couldn't help but smile inwardly at his devotion to his paper route.

"I'll call the paper and let them know what happened." She tipped her chin toward the hall. "I'll be up in a few minutes. And pull out your duffel bag."

Kerri shifted her focus to Wade as she spoke her next words. "You and I are going to take a little trip."

Tom frowned, but asked no questions, his footfalls pounding up the stairs a moment later.

Wade stepped close and Kerri took a backward step, having no desire to be physically near the man. What little warmth she'd felt toward him earlier vanished, chilled by the dangerous situation into which he'd tossed her son.

"What do you think you're doing?" A mix of frustration and concern blazed in his eyes.

"Getting my son as far away from here as possible." The fury in her voice startled her.

Wade narrowed his dark gaze. "You don't even know what happened."

She shook her head. "I don't need to know. It's plastered all over your face. Someone tried to run him down, didn't they?"

Wade winced again, guilt washing across his tense features. He nodded. "I'm sorry."

"Sorry?" Kerri's voice rose sharply and she hoped Tom had closed his bedroom door. "You're sorry someone tried to run down my son. He could have been killed, am I right?"

Wade hesitated, his gaze searching her face, gentle now. She ignored the sudden desire to let her anger soften beneath the sincerity of his stare.

He nodded.

Kerri moved to push past him, but he hooked one of

her elbows in his grasp. She pressed her lips tightly together, fighting the urge to shove him away.

"The police will protect you. You can't run. Whoever this is will find you. Let me help you."

"Help us?" She jerked her arm free of his grasp. "This family has no need for your help. I can take care of my own son, apparently far better than you can."

"Let me go talk to McCann."

"McCann? What has he done to protect us? Obviously not enough." She leaned close, anger heating her cheeks. "Someone in that department leaked Tom's identity and you want to go back there for help? What's wrong with you, Wade?"

He straightened as if she'd slapped him. "Maybe I was wrong to drag Tom into this."

"You're damned right you were wrong. Now it's up to me to get him out of this. We're leaving town for however long it takes."

His strong features tightened with worry. "Where will you go?"

"It's better that I don't tell you," Kerri answered, leaving out the fact she had absolutely no idea about where to go. "If you don't know, you can't tell anyone."

One dark brow lifted. "You don't know where you're going, do you?"

Damn the man. He'd been able to see right through her since the day they'd met. She forced a weak smile and tipped her chin. "Don't I?"

Wade turned for the door. "I'll be back in an hour."

He gave her a long look over his shoulder. "Do not leave until I come back. Promise me, Red."

Kerri nodded in an effort to hasten his departure. The sooner he was in his truck and out of her drive, the sooner she could throw together some clothes and food, grab her son and leave town.

She had no idea of where they were going or for how long, but every instinct she possessed screamed loud and clear. As long as they stayed where they were, Tom was in danger, and that was a reality she wasn't willing to accept.

She had no plans to wait for Wade's return.

Not now.

Not ever.

WADE DIDN'T WAIT for Adam McCann to wave him over to his desk, instead storming across the precinct floor. McCann's eyes narrowed as Wade neared, and he held up a finger while he cut his phone conversation short.

Wade leaned over the desk, dropping his voice so low only McCann could hear. "You want to tell me who on your team leaked word of the Nelson boy being a witness?"

McCann's eyes narrowed further still. "What are you talking about?"

"Someone called Kerri last night and threatened her to keep her son away from the police."

"Damn it." McCann reached for the phone. "I'll put someone at the house—"

"Not good enough," Wade interrupted and leaned closer still. "Someone tried to run that boy down this morning."

Now he had McCann's full attention. "What the hell are you talking about?"

"Out on his paper route. A beat-up old van came right at him, and the boy had nowhere to go. If I hadn't gotten there when I did, you'd have no witness."

McCann said nothing.

"She's taking him and running," Wade continued.

"Then you've got to stop her."

"Do I?"

Did he?

He wanted to put away whoever had destroyed Pine Ridge, but Tom Nelson's safety had to come first. Surely there was a way to achieve both. "You've got to find your leak and shut it down."

McCann's features twisted with annoyance. "I thought I could trust everyone here. It's not someone on my team. You can be sure of that."

Wade arched his eyebrows, saying nothing.

"Look," McCann continued, "it won't happen again. Unless they've got a bug in my desk, this conversation goes no further than here." He rapped his knuckles against the battered metal desk.

"What we need to do is relocate them." McCann reached for a phonebook. "There's a hotel we use all the time—"

"Not good enough," Wade interrupted. "I want them as far away as possible."

His gaze locked with McCann's and held for a long beat.

"She's going to run." Wade pressed his lips together before he continued. "It's up to you. Either do as I ask, or lose your witness."

"They're still looking at you, you know." McCann smiled wryly. "How do I know this isn't all some act to cover up insurance fraud?"

Anger seethed through Wade. "You're kidding me, right?"

"Am I?" The lines of McCann's smile deepened, infuriating Wade.

"I don't have time for your bull, McCann. Kerri and her son are in danger. Either you help me, or I'll take matters into my own hands."

"Aren't you the one who dragged them into the investigation to begin with?"

McCann's words rang true and Wade drew in a slow breath. "That's why I'm responsible for seeing them through this. Safely."

McCann nodded. "All right." He pulled a ring of keys out of his desk drawer and twisted a single key free. "I've got an idea. Old cabin up in the Poconos." He held the key out toward Wade.

"Used to be my dad's," McCann continued. "Haven't been there in a while, so I can't vouch for the condition of the place, but at least it's something."

Wade wrapped his fingers around the key, pressing the cold metal into his palm. "What guarantee do I have that they'll be safe there?"

McCann glanced around the room, and Wade's gaze followed. The place was quiet, with the few detectives present focused intently on case files or computer screens.

"I'd say you're pretty safe," McCann answered.

But as Wade settled back into the driver's seat of his pickup he knew he had to remain vigilant, no matter what McCann said.

If Tom's identity had leaked, surely their location might, as well.

KERRI WAITED impatiently while Tom gathered up his handheld video game paraphernalia. She longed to scream at him that hurrying might just be a matter of life and death, but she was determined not to let on as to why they were fleeing their home.

She glanced at the clock. Forty-five minutes since Wade had left. She wanted to be long gone before he returned.

The last thing she needed was a protector—especially Wade Sorenson.

She fingered the amethyst heart she'd tucked into her pocket at the last moment.

Sentimental fool.

There'd been a time years earlier when she'd considered the stone her lucky talisman. Well, she and Tom could use all the luck they could get now.

During the days following John's death and during Wade's testimony against her husband, she'd kept the heart in her pocket at all times.

She knew it was ridiculous to empower an inanimate object with such importance, but if nothing else, the heart had given her something to hold on to when there had been nothing else solid in her life.

Tom pounded down the stairs and Kerri breathed a sigh of relief.

"All set?" She worked to keep the tension she felt out of her tone, but Tom squinted at her just the same.

"You all right, Mom?"

"Sure." She ruffled his hair. "It's just not every day your son almost gets run off the road."

"Wait until I tell everyone when school's back in session."

"Mmm."

She steered Tom toward the door as she reached for her weekender bag. She stole a glance at the door to her studio and realized she had no idea how long they'd be gone.

She'd been working for weeks on a commissioned sculpture for a Philadelphia couple.

"Hang on a sec."

Kerri pushed the front door closed and hurried toward her studio, wanting to grab her address book. If their little adventure lasted more than a few days, she'd never be able to deliver the sculpture as promised, but her son's life was more important than any job.

If she had to, she'd find a way to pay back the

advance she'd already spent on this month's mortgage and groceries.

She shook herself from her thoughts.

What did it matter? Paying back the money was the least of her concerns right now.

Tom was all that mattered.

She slipped the small leather book into her bag and headed back toward the front door. "Let's hurry up. I want to get on the road before the afternoon traffic picks up."

Kerri tossed their bags into the trunk, checked the boxes of nonperishable food she'd positioned on the backseat, then dropped into the driver's seat, slamming the door closed behind her. She pushed the automatic door lock button even before she cranked on the ignition.

"Where are we going, Mom?"

Where were they going?

Kerri had no idea. "It's a surprise," she answered.

To you and me both.

She pressed the accelerator and sped down their drive, slamming on the brakes when Wade's dark green pickup skidded to a stop in her path.

He glared at her through the windshield and she knew there'd be no talking him out of going with them.

Her hot anger tempered at the intensity of his expression, and she realized that—as much as she was loathe to admit it—a small part of her felt relief at Wade's arrival.

Deep inside, she didn't want to be alone in fighting to keep Thomas safe. There was a part of her that longed for the days when Wade's presence in her home had been an almost daily—and welcome—occurrence.

Yet deep inside was an even larger part she couldn't ignore.

The part that knew no matter how kind Wade acted toward her son, no matter how protective and caring he appeared, the man was responsible for her husband's death.

For Tom's father's death.

No amount of protection in the world was going to smooth over that scar.

Chapter Five

Kerri breathed a sigh of relief as a small cabin came into view through the thick pines. Wade steered her car along the narrow dirt road, pulling to a stop in an overgrown turnaround.

They'd driven in silence.

Utter silence.

Poor Tom had tried to make conversation when they'd started out. He'd brought along a pile of detective novels, as usual.

When he wasn't playing video games or skateboarding, her son loved nothing more than to bury his nose in a book. She could think of far worse things for him to enjoy.

The problem was that Tom now fancied himself an expert on solving mysteries. He'd babbled excitedly about ecoterrorism until he realized the two adults in the car weren't joining in the conversation.

Guilt eased through Kerri just thinking about it.

She'd have to ask him to explain it all to her later to make up for her silence in the car.

He'd just about jumped out of his skin with excitement when Wade climbed into their car and announced he'd be traveling with them.

Kerri didn't have the heart to tell her son she'd like nothing more than to kick his Uncle Wade to the curb.

Wade pulled the car to a stop next to the cabin, cut the ignition and studied her for a moment, his dark eyes intense, no nonsense.

A chill rippled through her and she wasn't sure at that moment whether the man represented protection or a threat in her mind.

"Ready?" Wade looked over his shoulder at Tom, plastering on a smile Kerri would peg as fake from a mile away. Tom, however, grinned in response to Wade's question and bounded out of the car.

Fear squeezed at her belly and she scrambled after her son. "Hold on. Let Uncle Wade go first."

What if someone already knew where they'd gone? What if someone had beaten them here? Or followed them?

After all, if these criminals were capable of trying to run her son down on their own road, they'd apparently stop at nothing to keep him from testifying against them.

"I've got him," Wade said softly as he hurried after Tom. "Ready to help me open this place up?" he called out.

Tom stood his ground, waiting as Kerri had asked

him, but the child literally vibrated inside his skin. Poor kid. He missed his father so much. Kerri knew the prospect of spending this time with Wade filled Tom with nothing but pure excitement.

As Wade and Tom disappeared inside the cabin, she popped the trunk and lifted out the linens she'd brought along. She left behind Tom's sleeping bag and a stack of folded towels.

Glancing at the cabin, regret whispered through her. She should have brought a trunkload of cleaning supplies. From the look of the place—its battered porch and dirt-encrusted windows—the cabin hadn't seen much in the way of tender loving care in a very long time.

Wade and Tom worked together to open windows, sweep the wood floor, shake out rugs and knock down cobwebs. Kerri couldn't help but notice how patient Wade was with her son—explaining every task as they performed it and encouraging Tom to participate hands-on.

Wade had a gentleness about him she'd always admired, even back in high school. He had a big heart, even though he did his best to hide it.

She shook the charitable thoughts out of her head. She wasn't about to soften where Wade Sorenson was concerned, even if she hadn't seen her son's eyes sparkle so brightly in a very long time.

A short while later, Kerri flipped the musty covers off the bed, and spread out one of her quilts from home. She'd used a spiderweb-covered broom to sweep the floor when Wade and Tom were outside turning on the water.

Even though they'd swept once, their idea of cleanliness left a lot to be desired.

Men.

She smiled in spite of herself.

Tom burst through the cabin door as she was wiping down the kitchen with a rag she'd found.

"Uncle Wade said to try the water."

Kerri moved to the sink and cranked open the spigot, wincing at the clanging the pipes made as they came back to life. Air burst from the faucet first, followed by brown water.

"Gross." Tom crinkled his nose.

Kerri chuckled. "It'll clear. You'll see."

Wade placed his hands on her shoulders and she tensed. She hadn't heard him come back in.

"Success?" he asked.

"You did it," Tom said, a grin spreading wide across his freckled face.

Kerri stepped clear of Wade's touch, making a show of moistening the rag and continuing her cleaning.

Tom placed his hands on his slender hips, took a visual inventory of the cabin's interior and frowned. "Didn't you bring my sleeping bag, Mom?"

Kerri forced a smile, not wanting anything to erase the look of innocent bliss plastered across her son's face. "In the trunk."

Tom spun on one heel, headed for the door, but Wade reached out for his shoulder. "I'll help you."

Tom's features twisted into a puzzled expression, but he shrugged and let Wade walk him outside.

A pang of anxiety teased at Kerri's insides. If Wade thought Tom needed an escort just to grab a sleeping bag from the trunk, how safe could this location be?

She moved to the doorway, watching the two as they gathered the rest of the items from the car. Warmth spread through her when Wade reached over to ruffle Tom's hair.

Myriad memories flooded through her mind. All the times they'd picnicked together, gone to ball games together, shared meals, shared laughs.

They'd lost all that in a blink of an eye—in the time it took for a cement floor to give way in a partially constructed casino parking garage.

"You okay?" Wade squeezed her elbow as he passed and Kerri instinctively yanked her arm free of his touch.

The surprised look on Tom's face told her she'd reacted too sharply. She'd have to be more careful.

Tom idolized Wade and she'd never had the heart to tell him the truth about what had happened after his father died. She wasn't about to tell him now—or ever—if she could help it.

Once the police apprehended the man who had attacked Pine Ridge, the threat to Tom would disappear. She and her son would be able to return to life just as they'd been living it.

Together.

Alone.

But as she looked at Wade and Tom working together to unfurl the sleeping bag, a sliver of longing wound through her for the way it once was, and never would be again.

They'd agreed that she and Tom would take the small bedroom while Wade slept on the battered sofa, so Tom happily settled in the bedroom to read one of his books. Wade had promised Tom they'd take a walk through the woods a bit later, and Kerri had suggested her son go read to pass the time while he waited.

Wade had gone outside to double-check the car locks, leaving Kerri alone in the living area. She scrutinized the cabin from one end to the other, spotting a pile of dirt she'd missed in the corner of the small kitchen.

"Great."

She dropped to her knees and swiped her rag across the surface, grimacing when the amethyst heart popped out of her pocket and hit the floor with a thunk.

"Damn," she muttered beneath her breath. She'd meant to tuck the piece somewhere safe while she cleaned.

She reached to retrieve the stone then sat back on her heels just as Wade's boots entered her line of vision.

"I can't believe you still have that." The note of surprise in his voice rang crystal clear.

Kerri wrapped her fingers around the heart and lifted her gaze to Wade's. His dark brows furrowed, his expression a mix of amusement and confusion.

"I wasn't sure you'd remember giving it to me."

His lips pressed into a tight line. "I remember."

Kerri shot him a weak smile and climbed to her feet, brushing a fine layer of dust from the knees of her jeans.

Wade held out his hand and Kerri pressed the amethyst into his palm. A relaxed smile spread wide across his face.

"I served up a lot of hamburgers to buy this for you."

"Why did you?"

"Serve hamburgers?" Amusement danced in his dark eyes.

Kerri shook her head. "You know what I meant."

Wade shrugged, but kept hold of the stone, turning it slowly in his palm, scrutinizing the play of light against the curves and facets. "It reminded me of you, I suppose. Pretty with a bit of a hard edge."

Kerri said what she'd always wanted to say before her brain kicked in to stop her. "I always thought you might be the one to ask me out."

She regretted the words as soon as she spoke.

Wade visibly flinched. Apparently he'd asked himself the same question a time or two.

"John beat me to it, if you really want to know."

Kerri's cheeks warmed and she mentally chastised herself for the reaction.

Wade reached out to give back the stone, but kept his hand on hers after he lowered the heart to her palm.

"I've always wondered what might have happened if I hadn't waited so long."

Kerri swallowed, her eyes never leaving Wade's. She didn't want to acknowledge the sideways tilt her stomach took, but there was no denying she'd wondered the same thing countless times over the years.

John had been a wonderful father, but she'd always wondered if there shouldn't have been more to their married life. More laughter. More talking. More love.

The silence between her and Wade morphed into a void. Wade closed the emotional space between them by lowering his mouth to Kerri's without warning.

She stiffened, but he never let go of her hand, nor did he break their kiss, pressing his tongue against her lips, parting them, tasting, tempting.

Kerri shook her head and took a backward step. She pressed her fingertips to her lips and blinked. What on earth were they doing?

"I wasn't responsible for John's death."

Wade's words broke through Kerri's trance and she turned, tripping over a loose floorboard, stumbling toward the cabin door.

"I need some air." She fingered the amethyst in her hand, resisting the urge to throw it at Wade.

How dare he kiss her!

How dare he bring up John's death in the midst of what they were going through, in the moment after he'd kissed her! As if kissing her would make her forgive him.

She dashed down the steps and past her car, heading into the woods, following a narrow, well-worn dirt path.

Wade didn't call out after her, nor did she hear any footsteps behind her.

Good.

She didn't want to hear another word from the man. Not another profession of innocence, or friendship, or caring.

He'd had his chance years ago, and he'd blown it. He'd had his chance to prove his friendship, but he'd chosen to save his own reputation by tarnishing John's memory.

She began to run, letting the downhill slope speed her pace, stumbling a bit, but regaining her balance. When the incline became too much for her and she was afraid she'd fall, Kerri caught herself by looping one arm around a sapling.

A rustle sounded in the woods behind her and she frowned.

Great.

Wade must have decided to follow her after all. Well, she had a thing or two to say to him and this time, he was going to listen.

But when she turned in the direction of the noise she'd heard, she saw nothing. No one.

"Wade?"

She was certain of what she'd heard. A definite movement.

"Wade?" she repeated.

She turned slowly, pivoting on her heel, searching the dense foliage around her.

When the rustling sounded again, the small hairs at the base of her neck pricked to attention.

Something—or someone—was definitely out there. The question was what—or *who?*

THE WOMAN TURNED, looking in his direction, and he reflexively pressed against the rough bark of a nearby tree. When she spun slowly around, obviously a bit afraid, he chuckled to himself.

He hadn't thought he'd take such pleasure in pursuing this family. Typically, his thrills came from the fires. From the ignition and the licking flames, the collapsing structures.

All for a good cause. The best cause. The sanctity of the environment.

At least that's what they'd told him when they'd hired him.

He'd developed quite a reputation for his ability to deliver the job and leave no incriminating evidence. Project Liberation had become his steadiest source of work.

Slinking through the forest behind the kid's mother filled him with a different sort of thrill. A deeper thrill. A more powerful thrill.

There was something sensual about her movements as she searched the woods, as her fear played out across her pretty features. His body responded, tightening, adrenaline pumping through his system.

He didn't plan to take her out, merely incapacitate her and draw Sorenson out of the cabin.

If everything went as planned, Sorenson would no doubt rush to the woman's aid, leaving the kid alone.

Then they'd take care of business. Once and for all. He'd felt guilty over the prospect before the botched hit-

and-run attempt. Now, he was just pissed. Pissed and ready to get rid of the witness once and for all.

He'd never been very good with guns, so he'd brought an associate along to take care of the kid. The guy had perfect aim.

Dead perfect.

He chuckled, catching himself too late.

"Wade?"

An unmistakable note of fear tinged the woman's voice now. He used the moment to move in closer, so close he could almost reach out and stroke her long, red hair.

When she spun on him, pinning him with her startled gaze, the reality of what he was about to do washed over him, power welling inside him. Growing. Taking over.

He smiled, then made his move.

WADE DIDN'T GO AFTER Kerri, knowing he'd screwed up royally. What in the hell had he been thinking?

He hadn't been thinking, that was the problem.

He'd seen the softening of her features when she'd asked why he'd never asked her out. His senses had snapped back to high school, forgetting the present, losing himself in the past. In what might have been.

He'd kissed her.

He shut his eyes momentarily.

What an idiot.

Here he was, supposedly focused on nothing but her

son's safety and he'd kissed the woman. Then he'd insisted on his innocence in John's death.

Again.

But he was innocent. John's death had been an accident—a tragic accident brought on by the man's own poor judgment.

A hollow ache tugged at Wade's insides.

John had been his best friend and Wade missed him, but he was also angry—sometimes angrier than hell. How could John make such an amateur mistake? And the accident *had* been due to John's error.

Wade was quickly growing sick and tired of the blame painted so blatantly across Kerri's face each time she looked at him.

He'd fought long and hard to prove that what had happened was no fault of his own. No fault of his company's.

He wasn't about to stop fighting now.

The Pine Ridge fires were doing nothing to help the reputation he'd fought so hard to rebuild. Damn McCann for even mentioning the phrase *insurance fraud.*

Wade would never do such a thing. He wasn't cut from that cloth. Never had been. Never would be.

"Uncle Wade?"

Tom's hesitant tone sliced clean through Wade's thoughts. He turned to find Tom standing in the middle of the room, features twisted with curiosity.

"Where'd Mom go?"

Wade dragged a hand across his eyes, stalling for a

split second. "Said she needed to stretch her legs. She'll be right back."

"What if the guy who tried to run me down followed us here? The bad guys do that all the time in my books." Worry creased his pale forehead. "Is she safe?"

Was she safe?

Trepidation filtered through Wade, and he gave thought to chasing after Kerri, but McCann had given his word. Their location would remain a secret.

And what had happened to Tom's thinking this morning's near-accident was a fluke?

"Who says that guy was trying to run you down?"

Tom rolled his eyes. "I didn't want to scare Mom, but he was coming straight for me." He shrugged. "They don't want me to testify, right? Just like in my books."

Just like in my books.

Only this was real life. Tom's life.

And he didn't want the kid living in fear.

Wade shook his head. "I still say it was an accident." He closed the gap between them and ruffled Tom's shaggy hair. "But stick close to me, just the same. Deal?"

Tom leaned against him, and Wade wrapped an arm around his slender shoulders, his gut tightening at the depth of emotion he felt for the boy. The emotion he felt for the boy *and* his mother.

If anything happened to either one of them, he'd… well…he'd kill whoever hurt them with his bare hands.

Plain and simple.

"We probably shouldn't tell Mom, right?" Tom asked. "She's got enough to worry about."

Wade smiled over the top of Tom's head. "Pretty smart for a nine-year-old, aren't you?"

But before Tom could answer, a scream shattered the quiet of the wooded surroundings outside.

A woman's scream.

Kerri's scream.

Wade was out the door, down the steps and racing through the dense foliage before his brain kicked into gear.

Tom.

He couldn't leave Tom alone. What if whatever had happened to Kerri was a diversion?

He spun around, colliding with Tom, who had obviously followed close on his heels.

He grasped the boy's shoulders. "Run the opposite way and hide."

"But that was Mom."

All color drained from Tom's face, and his pale eyes grew larger than Wade had ever seen them. The kid was terrified.

"Just do it." Wade gave him a quick shake. "I'll take care of your mom, I promise." He released his grip then pressed a hand to Tom's chest. "Run."

"But—"

Wade said what he hadn't wanted to say. "You were right when you said that van almost hitting you wasn't an accident."

Understanding snapped into focus in Tom's eyes.

"Run and hide," Wade repeated.

He waited just long enough to be sure Tom was headed in the opposite direction and away from the cabin before he turned, racing toward Kerri's scream.

There had been no sound, no scream, no anything since her first scream.

Maybe she'd fallen and twisted an ankle or hit her head. Maybe the terror in her voice had been due to something other than someone out to harm her.

Whatever the case might be, Wade was certain of one thing above all else.

He'd do whatever he had to do to keep Kerri safe.

He could only pray he wasn't too late.

Chapter Six

Kerri froze in disbelief at the face before her, not Wade, yet someone she'd seen somewhere. Wasn't it?

He backhanded her before she could react and she hit the ground with an unforgiving thud, pine needles and dirt filling her mouth and nostrils.

She scrambled forward, working to get enough of a foothold to propel herself away from her attacker, but he grabbed her ankles and pulled her back toward him.

Her heart hammered in her chest, fear slicing through her. Surely her life couldn't end like this, could it? And what would happen to Tom if her attacker did away with her now? Who would take care of him, protect him, raise him?

Wade's face flashed through her mind and she suddenly wished he had followed her out onto the path. If only she'd been with him, this guy wouldn't have dared his daylight assault.

Kerri knew she had to do something to break her attacker's hold. She kicked frantically, rejoicing at the man's loud swearing when one foot slipped out of his grip then connected with his hand.

He lost his hold on her other foot and she scrambled to her feet, unable to ignore her throbbing cheekbone. She turned to run, but her attacker grabbed her hair, pulling her back.

She screamed with every ounce of strength she held inside.

It was now or never. If she couldn't attract Wade's attention, there was no doubt about it. Her attacker was too big and too strong for her to escape.

The man looped one arm around her neck and spun her to face him, mercilessly slamming the back of his hand across her face again. He struck her a third time before her knees buckled and she sank to the dirt, the world around her spiraling out of focus.

Everything grew dimmer—sight and sound—just as Wade's voice broke through, penetrating the numb fog that had taken up residence inside her brain.

"Kerri! Kerri!"

"Get Tom," she murmured into the pine needles and dirt.

"Don't worry. I will." Her attacker's voice sounded close to her ear and she shuddered, fear for her son ripping through her.

"No."

But he was gone, moving away, his footsteps fading fast.

"Kerri!"

Wade's voice grew nearer now. Closer.

"Tom," she whispered. "Get Tom."

Her attacker's footfalls faded completely while Wade's grew louder, coming from the direction of the cabin.

Hold on.

She had to hold on.

She had to tell Wade to get Tom. Get him far away. Where no one could touch him.

But her mental fog thickened, pulling her under, pulling her down into the dark, deep abyss of unconsciousness before she could utter another word.

WADE SEARCHED FRANTICALLY, listening for the slightest sound, for an answer to his calls.

A figure broke through the trees and raced away from him. He moved to give chase, but knew he had to find Kerri. Had to make sure she was all right.

He saw her then, her red hair splayed against the forest floor, her figure sprawled in an awkward position, her body without movement.

No.

"Kerri!"

Wade raced to her, dropping to his knees, skidding to a stop beside her. He checked first for a pulse, breathing a huge sigh of relief when he found the rhythm, steady and strong.

"Kerri."

As he called her name, he ran his hands gently over her, searching for any sign of major damage. She was scratched and bloody, yet nothing appeared to be broken. Her face had begun to swell where she'd obviously been struck and cut more than once, perhaps the reason she'd passed out.

"Tom," she murmured.

Wade's gut caught and twisted. He gathered her gently into his arms, afraid to worsen any injury he hadn't spotted.

Kerri's eyes blinked open. "Tom," she repeated.

"He's fine." Wade nodded, trying to muster his most confident expression. Truth was, if someone were capable of doing this to Kerri—who hadn't seen a thing at Pine Ridge—he didn't want to consider what that same person might do to Tom.

"Where?" Kerri grimaced as she worked to sit up, worked to move out of Wade's arms.

"I told him to run and hide—to head in the opposite direction." He helped Kerri sit upright, then let go of her trembling body as much as he wanted to bundle her close and soothe her battered spirit. "Even if they search the cabin, they won't find him."

Her expression eased slightly just as a gunshot rang out. Then a second. A third.

Their eyes locked as if they'd been suspended in a shared thought between denial and the realization that shots had been fired in the same direction into which Wade had instructed Tom to run.

Kerri mouthed the word *no* as Wade helped her scramble to her feet.

"Are you—"

But she was off and running before Wade could finish his question.

KERRI RACED THROUGH the foliage, nowhere near anything resembling a path, small tree limbs and tall weeds slapping against her body, snagging into her jeans and her sleeves. A heavy lock of hair had plastered itself to her face and she frantically wiped it away, doing her best to ignore the sticky wetness that covered her cheek.

Blood, no doubt. Her blood.

She ran as fast as she could, well aware Wade was just behind her, following her through the dense foliage. He grasped her arm, urging her to let him pass.

"Let me go first."

He didn't have to say the words *just in case,* she could read them in his eyes.

Kerri nodded, slowing only enough to let him get by, then matching him stride for stride as they raced toward the direction of the shots.

Her body protested, battered and sore, but she didn't care. She couldn't care. She had to find Tom. Any injury she might have sustained could wait.

Her heart raced uncontrollably, and when a figure appeared, facedown in the dust and pine needles, Kerri stopped in her tracks, frozen momentarily at the horrible possibility the body might be Tom's.

"Too big," Wade called out over his shoulder. "Get down."

She did as he asked, ducking next to a large tree trunk, watching as he carefully approached the lifeless form, checking for a pulse then shaking his head.

Her heart tumbled to her stomach.

Who was this person? Where was her son?

My God, had he been kidnapped?

Her attacker had taken off in the opposite direction hadn't he? Was it possible that not only had this second man been near the cabin but that a third person might have fired the shots? But who? Someone McCann had sent for protection?

A small hand pressed to her shoulder and she fell to her side, scared half to death by the sudden movement.

Tom's pale, frightened face was a welcomed sight and she wrapped her arms around him and squeezed.

"Are you all right?"

He nodded against her shoulder, but made no effort to hide his sobbing, so unlike her son.

Damn whoever was behind this, whoever had put such fear into her son's heart. Into her heart.

She'd stop at nothing to keep Tom safe.

Nothing.

Wade quickly moved back to where she and Tom huddled together. He pulled off his T-shirt, gently wiping at Kerri's face as she held her son. She realized what he was doing, and gave him a quick look of appreciation.

Tom hadn't yet spotted her injuries.

The less he saw, the better.

Tears swam in her eyes, but she blinked them back. This was no time to show weakness, no time to show fear. Tom needed her to be strong, and she'd be damned if she'd let Wade see her appear weak.

"It's not the guy who attacked me," she said to Wade.

He glanced back at the body. "I think I recognize him from the mug shots. Think he's a Project Liberation regular."

"He's not the man who set the fires."

Tom spoke as he lifted his head and Kerri turned his cheek, forcing him to look away from the body.

"I saw him when he was chasing me," he continued. "Before he got shot."

Kerri shuddered. Her son could have been killed.

"Who fired the shot?" she asked Wade.

He frowned, worry snapping his eyebrows together.

Cold chills wrapped themselves around Kerri's spine, and she pulled Tom to his feet.

"Let's go. We're packing up and getting out of here."

"Where to, Mom?"

She drew in a deep breath and shook her head. She hadn't the slightest idea.

She looked at Wade, instantly recognizing the familiar, fierce determination in his expression.

"I know just the place," he said.

"That's what—"

He held up a hand to stop her before she could say anything more. "This is different. This time, no one knows but the three of us. No one."

TEN MINUTES LATER, they were packed and on the road, leaving dust and dirt swirling behind them as they barreled away from the cabin.

Wade put a call in to McCann describing the location and condition of the body. When asked if he'd sent an officer to protect them, McCann told Wade he hadn't, and he had no idea who the shooter might have been if it hadn't been Kerri's attacker.

The possibilities chilled Wade to the bone.

Were they dealing with Project Liberation? Or something else? Something even bigger?

McCann told him to sit tight until the investigative team showed up, but Wade simply hung up and turned off his phone.

He could feel the heat of Kerri's anger stretching across the console between them. He couldn't blame her. If he hadn't insisted on Tom coming forward, she and her son would no doubt be home safe and sound right now.

He glanced quickly toward the backseat. Tom had fallen asleep instantly, emotionally and physically wrung dry.

"We need to make a stop," Wade said softly, so as not to wake Tom.

"No." Kerri shook her head. "We need to get wherever we're going and fast. Then we need to stay hidden."

Wade reached out to touch her face, but she turned away.

"We've got to get you cleaned up. See how bad it is."

She waved a hand dismissively. "I don't need you to take care of me."

"Like hell," he muttered, refocusing on the road. He didn't care what Kerri wanted or didn't want. He planned to stop for supplies and tend to her wounds.

A short while later he did just that, hitting a fast-food drive-thru at the same time. Tom hungrily wolfed down a huge hamburger in the backseat while Wade dabbed at Kerri's battered cheek.

She winced with each touch. "Do you think it's broken?" she whispered.

Wade shrugged. "Hard to say without an X-ray."

Kerri grimaced. "Then I guess we'll never know."

As they took off down the road, Kerri held her own hamburger in her lap, untouched. Wade's sandwich still sat in the bag.

Perhaps the grim reality of their situation had taken hold of Kerri's thoughts as much as it had his. When they shared a quick glance, he was sure of it.

Anger and fear tangled for position in Kerri's eyes.

He planned to make damn sure she'd have need for neither emotion once he got her and Tom safely hidden away.

KERRI AND TOM scrunched down in the car as Wade paid for the one-room efficiency. Kerri sneaked a glance but could only hear, not see, the surf as it crashed against the far side of the boardwalk under the cover of darkness.

Wildwood, New Jersey.

She could barely remember the last time she'd been here.

The sound of children's laughter, parents' voices and the music of boardwalk carnival rides carried her back to summers past.

The warm August air filtered in through the open windows, tinged heavily with the tang of the salty ocean.

"Can we go on a ride, Mom?" Tom asked.

"Not tonight, honey."

"When?"

When?

Whenever the person—or persons—who want you silenced are behind bars.

"I'm not sure." She shook her head and forced a smile. "Maybe tomorrow."

Appeased, Tom sank back down into the seat and said nothing else until they'd unpacked the car and settled into their tiny efficiency.

Kerri longed to have some time alone with Wade— time to tell him exactly what was on her mind. He'd not only thrust her son into harm's way, but he'd dredged up the past with his kiss and his words.

I wasn't responsible for John's death.

How dare he?

Anger, attraction and dismay swirled inside her. She shoved a hand through her hair as she unfurled Tom's sleeping bag.

She didn't have time to worry about Wade now. She needed to focus on keeping Tom safe until the authorities had things under control. She needed to keep her wits about her, and that included reining in the need to hash out unresolved issues with Wade.

She simply couldn't afford to waste either the time or the energy listening to—or arguing with—anything the man had to say.

After they'd unpacked the car, Wade headed out with the promise of finding something cool for them to drink.

Nervousness skittered through Kerri as she and Tom waited for his return. Kerri had taken an inventory of the tiny efficiency kitchen and had found it nicely stocked with the necessary cooking utensils. Now all she needed to do was put together a meal from the boxes she'd hastily packed.

Tom had asked again about the boardwalk. Poor kid. She knew it was torture for him to be so close, yet unable to explore. He understood they were in hiding, but she was certain he didn't understand the magnitude of the danger.

When the room's phone rang, she just about jumped out of her skin, reaching out a hand to stop Tom before he lifted the receiver.

"What if it's Wade?" His pale eyes widened.

Kerri shook her head. "He knows we wouldn't answer." She pulled the cord from the phone jack. "How's your video game coming?"

Tom happily refocused on the electronic game on his lap. "I made it to level four."

"Wow." She turned to finish unpacking the boxes of

food, doing her best to breathe slowly, hoping to slow the rapid beat of her heart.

Who would have called the room? Surely it had been a mistake. Probably meant for whoever had just checked out.

When Wade reentered the efficiency, Tom pounced before Kerri could ask the question.

"Did you call?"

Wade's eyes narrowed, his focus shifting to Kerri.

"The phone rang," she explained. She tipped her chin toward the dangling cord. "It won't happen again."

Wade plunked three cans of cola and a small paper bag on the well-worn, yellow Formica table and crossed to the phone. He inserted the line into the phone jack and punched three keys on the dial pad.

"Blocked," he muttered. He replaced the receiver and yanked the cord from the wall. "Thought I might be able to get the number that called, but the service is blocked."

Kerri nodded, disappointed in herself. She hadn't even thought to try.

"I made it to level four," Tom said, not even looking up from his game.

A crooked grin eased across Wade's mouth and he ruffled Tom's hair. Kerri smiled at the warm gesture, but straightened her features before Wade glanced in her direction.

"I'm starving." Wade blew out a breath and stretched. "And tired. Long drive."

"Well," Kerri turned back to the kitchen counter where she'd gathered a few items. "You're in for a treat. Macaroni and cheese for our main course and green beans for our side dish."

Wade nodded, one dark eyebrow arched. "Perfect. That ought to leave plenty of time for this." He dumped out the contents of the paper bag. Two boxes of hair color tumbled onto the tabletop.

Kerri frowned. "What's that for?"

"For you and Tom." He rubbed his chin, studying her. "I figured going darker would be easier than going lighter with your hair, Red."

Kerri winced at his use of the nickname, but fingered a strand of her trademark red hair. Wade had a point. The men who were after them had gotten good looks at both her and Tom. Changing hair color wasn't just smart, it was necessary.

She turned back to the kitchen, pulling a pot from beneath the cupboard. "All right then. Let's get this show on the road."

HE COULDN'T HELP but smile at the comfortable chatter that passed between mother and son as Kerri darkened Tom's hair. She'd done well raising the boy without John. That much was evident.

He'd missed spending time with both of them since the accident. Sure, he'd done his best to shove their images out of his head, but the shadows of memory were always there. Pressing in. Waiting to appear.

Wade had been so caught up in proving there had been no negligence on the part of his company, he'd jumped on the chance to vindicate the Sorenson Construction name—by testifying to John Nelson's carelessness.

His friend knew better. Knew the necessary waiting time after pouring concrete, yet still he'd urged the crew to get back to work. In the end, it had been John who had paid the price for his mistake.

Now Wade found himself in a hauntingly similar situation. He'd thrust Tom front and center on the Project Liberation radar screen by insisting he testify. Yes, he wanted justice for the family of the inspector who had died. But he also wanted to keep his company name in the clear.

Hell, even McCann had tossed out the idea of insurance fraud.

Wade squeezed his eyes shut and swore silently. He'd never do such a thing. Never.

His honor and his company's reputation meant everything to him. Everything. But he'd never imagined the lengths to which Project Liberation would go to keep Tom quiet.

Now it was up to him to make sure the boy stayed safe until he could testify. Then they'd all be happy. Tom and Kerri could go back to their lives and Wade's reputation would remain intact.

The solution was simple.

But as he watched mother and son look into each other's eyes, unable to mask the fear behind their smiles, Wade knew there was nothing simple at all about the solution.

Not a blessed thing.

Chapter Seven

They sat and clicked on the local news after Kerri and Tom finished coloring their hair. There was no mention of the shooting up in the mountains. McCann must have put a lid on any media coverage.

Tom fell asleep almost instantly and Wade lifted him effortlessly, carrying him into the bedroom, wondering how many times John had carried his son to bed. A sudden wave of regret hit him full force—much larger than what he'd felt earlier that night.

As he pulled the bedroom door shut behind him and turned back toward the living area, he mentally prepared himself for the wrath he knew Kerri had been holding at bay all evening.

She didn't disappoint.

"Do you want to tell me what happened today?" Daggers shot from her gaze, all the more vivid now in contrast to her newly dyed hair.

"They must have followed us."

"What about Detective McCann? He knew where we were going."

Wade shook his head. "You can trust him. I've known him for years."

He shrugged, asking himself the question he'd been mulling over all day. How *did* the men find them at the Pocono cabin?

"Maybe someone overheard us talking."

Kerri's angry expression intensified. "Maybe isn't good enough, Wade, and you know it. We need to know how this happened. Who's to say we weren't followed here?"

He drew in a slow breath, working to keep his own anger under control. He was stymied by their circumstances and he didn't want to take his frustration out on Kerri.

"I think I'd know if we were being followed."

Kerri's only response was a lift of her eyebrows.

Wade's simmering anger began to boil. "I know what I'm doing."

Her expression shifted to one far more serene, yet serious. "You've always known what you were doing, haven't you, Wade?"

Now she'd gone too far. He closed the gap between them and grasped her shoulders. "I am not responsible for John's death. He brought it on himself. I have the proof. You just refuse to listen."

Kerri stood her ground, not softening the slightest bit beneath his touch. If anything, she pulled herself straighter, taller.

"My family was destroyed three years ago, Wade. I'm counting on you to keep what's left of my family intact. Understood?"

He released his hold on her and took a backward step. "Understood."

She jerked a thumb toward the bedroom door. "That boy in there thinks the world of you. Don't let him down again."

Again.

Wade blinked, holding his tongue. They had to move past this if they were going to work together to keep Tom safe.

"I adore that kid, Red. You know that. I'd do anything for him. Anything for you. Don't you know that?"

Her stare never wavered—never left his face—yet she said nothing. She merely turned her back and took a step toward the bathroom.

"No." Wade reached out and hooked her arm, spinning her around. "What's it going to take before you forgive me for something I didn't even do?"

Tears welled in her eyes, taking Wade by surprise. If there was one thing he knew about Kerri it was that she didn't like to appear weak.

"I trusted you." She said, her voice barely more than a whisper. "You were our friend. *My* friend."

"I still am."

She looked so shaken, so vulnerable, he barely recognized her from the girl he'd once known—the girl with the light in her eyes and fire in her spirit.

The overwhelming need to protect her, to comfort her, overtook him. He brought his mouth down over hers, this time not backing off when she tensed. When she locked her arms around his neck and wound her fingers through his hair, his stomach caught and twisted. Hard.

Just as quickly as she'd softened, she tensed, sliding her hands to his chest and pushing him away, putting space between them.

She shook her head. "I can't do this."

"Kerri—"

She sucked in her lower lip, as if tasting the lingering effects of their kiss. "Whatever might have once been between us is gone." She squeezed her eyes shut momentarily and a lone tear slid down one cheek. "I have to go cut my hair now."

She took a few steps toward the bathroom then stopped, looking back over one shoulder. "I'm going to do everything in my power to keep my son's location a secret. I'd like to think I can trust you to do the same."

KERRI COULD TELL by the hurt plastered across Wade's expression that her words had hit home.

He stood, silently watching her as she stepped into the bathroom and stood before the mirror, lifting the pair of kitchen shears she'd found in the utensil drawer.

She hesitated, staring at her reflection in the mirror.

Her face was battered and swollen, angry purple and

black bruises marring the area over her cheekbone and beneath her eye.

Nausea roiled inside her.

She could have been killed.

Tom could have been killed.

What on earth had they gotten themselves into?

Her heartbeat hammered in her ears, her conflicted thoughts about Wade and her genuine fear for her son tangling for position inside her.

She studied her hair and swallowed, holding up a handful of the long, dyed brown strands.

Red.

Maybe now Wade would finally stop calling her by the nickname. Her traitorous belly caught and twisted.

Kerri shoved the thought out of her mind and scanned her reflection again.

Even without cutting her hair, she looked nothing like herself.

Hell, even her own mother wouldn't recognize her right now, but she couldn't be too careful. Not when it came to ensuring Tom's safety.

She sucked in a deep breath and cut, wincing as the length came away free in her hand.

Kerri repeated the process, section by section, until dark hair piled in the sink and a short, choppy cut framed her face.

She looked ridiculous. As much as she hated to admit it, she was going to need Wade's help.

As if he'd read her mind, he stepped behind her,

meeting her gaze in the mirror. She swallowed, not wanting to respond to the warmth of his body so close to hers.

He took the shears from her hand and began trimming at the ragged cut, patiently working his way around her head, section by section. His gentle touch sent chills dancing back and forth across her shoulders.

When he pressed his palm to her shoulder to turn her slightly, heat spread outward from his touch, reaching deep inside to a part of her that had gone cold a long time ago—years before John's death.

A shiver traced its way down her spine and her pulse quickened. Wade continued smoothing her haircut, his touch gentle, working silently.

If she didn't know better, Kerri would swear he was unaffected by their nearness, yet when their eyes met for a second time in the mirror, desire shone blatantly in his reflection.

She wanted to believe him—wanted to believe that he hadn't lied to protect his company. But did that make her disloyal to John? If she believed Wade, then she was accepting John's carelessness had caused his own death, and her husband had been anything but careless.

Matter of fact, he'd grown so controlling he'd been devoid of emotion by the time he died.

Wade's belief that John was at fault made no sense. No sense at all.

Conflict swirled inside her, tangling with her longing to move away from the past, to leave the heartache of her cold marriage and her husband's death behind once and for all.

When Wade set the shears down on the sink and grasped her shoulders, she didn't flinch, didn't lean away. If anything, she relaxed into his touch, wanting to forget the past. Truth be told, right now she wanted to forget the present.

She wanted to escape, to leave her fears behind, if only for tonight.

Wade dropped a kiss to her neck and she inhaled sharply, her every nerve ending springing to life. He ran his fingers up into her newly shorn hair and his caress sent shimmers of awareness scorching through her.

She should push him away. She should tell him to stop. But it had been so long since she'd lost herself to a lover's touch she didn't have the strength to say no when all she wanted to do was say yes.

Wade skimmed his fingers over her shoulders and down her arms. He slid his hands around her waist and pulled her tight, pressing his hard chest against her back.

She lifted her gaze to his in the mirror, excitement rippling through her at the heat she saw burning there.

Wade slid his palms over her ribs, lightly grazing the swells of her breasts with his thumbs. Kerri inhaled sharply, splaying her hands on either side of the sink to steady herself.

Wade lowered his mouth to her neck once again, tracing the lower edge of her hair where it brushed against her skin. Kerri dropped her chin, exposing the full expanse of her neck.

He trailed light kisses down to the curve of her shoulder, then stepped back and spun her around, pulling her body tight to his. Chest to chest. Stomach to stomach.

Kerri's breath caught.

"I don't want to make you do something you'll regret tomorrow."

Kerri pressed a finger to his lips. "Just make me feel."

He covered her mouth with his, teasing her lips apart then tasting deeply, exploring, teasing.

Heat spiraled inside Kerri's belly, tightening into a frantic coil of need. She'd been dead inside for so long the magnitude of her body's response frightened her, excited her.

All these years, she'd wondered what it would feel like to be in Wade's arms, to feel his hands on her body. As he skimmed his fingers along her sides, encircling her waist, then cupping her buttocks and pressing her tight against his erection, she had her answer.

His hands felt like magic, waking every inch of her body from its long slumber.

When he hoisted her into his arms, she made no sound of protest, instead leaning into him, dropping her own kisses to his neck, exploring the heat of his skin with her tongue, her lips, her fingertips.

Suddenly, she wanted all of him, wanted to know every inch of him, like she'd never known John, like she'd never known anyone.

He lowered her to the battered sofa then dropped to his knees beside her, pushing up the hem of her T-shirt to expose her bare flesh. He traced the back of his knuckles against her skin, pushing the shirt higher and higher until he brushed against the cotton of her bra.

Her skin blazed beneath his touch and she arched her back, wanting to feel his fingers against her for as long as possible.

Wade leaned close, pressing his mouth to her ear. "I've dreamt about this since the moment I first saw you."

Reality edged a bit at Kerri's sense of pleasure. "Then why—"

His kiss stopped her midquestion. Why had he never done anything? Never pursued her?

When he slid his hand beneath the wire of her bra and cupped her breast, all questions about the past evaporated. Suddenly all that mattered was the here and now. She and Wade. Nothing more.

He popped the clasp on her bra, exposing her naked flesh to the cool, air-conditioned air.

Kerri drew in a sharp breath and he raked his fingernail across her nipple, back and forth while she writhed beneath his touch.

When he lowered his mouth to her breast, suckling her flesh into his hot, wet mouth, a moan escaped from somewhere deep inside her. She pressed a hand to her mouth, not wanting to wake Tom.

Wade slid his hands behind her back, burying his

face in the valley between her breasts, trailing his tongue to the waistband of her jeans.

He popped open the button and lowered the zipper, helping her as she shimmied out of the denim, leaving her wearing nothing but a pair of her favorite cotton bikinis. He wasted no time in easing the soft fabric down her legs and over her ankles.

Her body pulsated with desire for him and she shivered, awed by the frenzied beat of her heart and the depth of her need for Wade.

She watched as he stepped out of his jeans and boxers in one fluid motion then lowered himself gently on top of her, his weight pressing against her, causing the sofa to moan and creak.

Kerri bit back a laugh, feeling suddenly like a schoolgirl about to lose her virginity—all nerves and excitement wrapped around her burning desire to feel Wade inside her.

She expected him to enter her, but he surprised her, pressing his mouth to her stomach, then nipping at her flesh, moving his kisses lower and lower until his tongue delved inside her.

She gasped, lifting her body to deepen the mind-blowing ecstasy of his tongue flicking and tasting, suckling and teasing.

Kerri thought she might lose her mind, she was so close to the edge of release. When Wade slipped one finger inside her, then two, all the while teasing her with his tongue, her body exploded with her orgasm, pulsating with her release.

But he didn't stop, running his hand up the flat of her belly to her breast, cupping her flesh, teasing her nipple as his mouth continued its hot exploration of her body. When Kerri's second orgasm peaked and crashed, the room spun with the intensity of her release.

Wade reached for his jeans, pulling his wallet out of his back pocket and flipping it open. When he extracted a foil package, Kerri groaned inwardly. She'd been so lost in Wade's lovemaking she'd never thought of protection.

Wade handed her the condom, asking her with no words, only a long, knowing look.

Kerri encircled his hard length, wrapping her fingers around the smooth, taut skin, slowly stroking down and then up. Down and then up.

When he drew a sharp breath through clenched teeth, she smiled, filled with a heady sense of power knowing her touch had ignited such longing. She positioned the condom and unrolled it, sheathing him completely.

He pressed another kiss to her neck, then her cheek, then closed his mouth over hers, delving deep, stealing her breath and leaving her wanting only more as he broke away.

Kerri bit back a moan, wanting so badly to feel Wade inside her. She'd almost forgotten her son slept in the next room, yet here she lay, making love to the man she'd once vowed to hate.

She wound her fingers through his short hair. "Now, Wade. Please."

Without a word, he raised himself above her, waiting

as she opened herself to him. He pressed his erection against her, probing, then easing gently inside.

He stroked slowly at first then more boldly, igniting the passion she'd kept locked inside until her body vibrated on the edge of release once more.

Wade slid his palms beneath her buttocks, angling her body to deepen their joining. He slowed, then quickened, then slowed, lifting his chin to meet her gaze, their stares holding, remaining locked until Kerri went over the edge.

She turned her face into one of the sofa's cushions to muffle her cries of pleasure as her body pulsated with yet another orgasm.

Wade shuddered and visibly bit back a moan, his release following immediately on the heels of Kerri's.

He lowered himself gently on top of her, enfolding her in his arms, whispering softly against her ear. "You are far more beautiful than I ever imagined."

Kerri absorbed his words without question, consumed with the sheer numbness of her pleasure. She had never had a sexual experience as intense or as intimate.

A sliver of doubt wormed its way into her consciousness, questioning whether what had just happened was merely the result of the day's life-threatening events.

She shoved the thought away, focusing instead on something she never thought she'd find herself considering.

As sleep began to overtake her senses, Kerri found herself wondering if tonight might signal a new beginning for her and Wade.

Could they ever be together?

Truly together?

But as the questions began to form in her mind, her spent body began to fade.

Her last thought as she slipped into sleep was that she felt loved.

And loved was something she hadn't felt in a very long time.

Chapter Eight

Wade's cell phone vibrated against the top of the end table and he pulled one arm from beneath Kerri to reach it. The pink glow of the sunrise eased around the room's cheap curtains.

Daybreak.

Who in the hell would call him this early?

"Yes." He answered sharply, hoping whoever was on the other end of the line would get the message their interruption was not appreciated.

"Nice mess you left up at the cabin." McCann sounded none too pleased.

Wade sat up, reaching for his shirt. "What did you expect us to do, sit around and wait for them to come back?"

"Where are you?"

"Nice try."

Wade dropped the phone to the floor and pulled his T-shirt over his head, then stepped into his jeans.

When he put the phone back to his ear, McCann was in midrant. "We're on the same side here—"

"Then tell me how those guys found us."

Kerri's eyes fluttered open. She pulled the blanket he'd covered her with after she'd fallen asleep up to her chin. He'd sat for a long while last night, staring at her, amazed at what had just happened.

He wasn't a fool. He knew she never would have weakened and made love to him under normal circumstances. She'd hated him for what she thought he'd done to John for too many years to let go. But maybe now things could be different. Once they survived the immediate threat.

If they survived the immediate threat.

Color flushed her cheeks and Wade gave her a smile, hoping that wasn't regret he saw painted across her lovely features.

She stood, pulling the blanket tightly around herself. She reached for her pile of clothes and headed for the bathroom. Wade waited until she was out of earshot to continue.

"Kerri Nelson took quite a beating out there. Whoever is behind this means business and apparently they don't care who gets in their way."

"We ID'd the body."

Wade scrubbed a hand across his face. "Project Liberation, right?"

"How did you know that?"

"Recognized him from shots you showed Tom." He

blew out a determined breath. "Any idea who the shooter was?"

"We're working on it." McCann paused, perhaps trying to be tactful, though knowing him as Wade did, he doubted it. "You need to get in here. Now. Enough is enough."

"Thanks, but no thanks." Wade stood and crossed to the window, pushing aside the curtain to catch the play of the vibrant sunrise against the ocean's surface. "When you get these guys behind bars we'll come in. Don't call me until then."

He moved to disconnect the call, but McCann's voice stopped him short. *What had he said?*

Wade pressed the phone back to his ear. "Repeat that."

"I knew I'd get your attention." McCann did nothing to hide the satisfaction in his voice. "I said we pulled in a known Project Liberation sympathizer and he fingered Michael Chase."

Michael Chase?

The rhythm of Wade's heartbeat quickened. Michael Chase was another of Wade's oldest friends. He was also the son of crime boss Vincent Chase.

Michael and Wade had grown up together, played together, gone to school together. Vincent Chase had been like a father to Wade after his own father died, treating him like a second son. He'd never pressed Wade to join the business. Matter of fact, he'd encouraged him to do anything but.

They'd lost contact during the years since Wade's

mother had moved the family to the southern part of the state, but Wade still found it difficult to believe Michael would have a thing to do with Project Liberation.

Why would he? A large chunk of the family money came from construction, and it was common knowledge construction was Project Liberation's favorite target.

"Doesn't make any sense." Wade's disbelief rang blatant in his tone.

"Got the guy's sworn statement. Your old buddy is a player in all this. Apparently, he's turned against his own family. I'd watch your back if I were you."

Wade rankled at McCann's implication. "He'd never turn against his father."

"You'd be surprised how often it happens." McCann made a snapping noise with his mouth. "I'll be in touch. In the meantime, give some thought to what I said. We can't protect the kid if we don't know where he is."

Kerri had emerged from the bathroom and stood fully dressed, studying Wade's face. She spoke the moment he disconnected the call.

"What was that all about?"

Wade stared at her, taking in her short brunette hair, the curiosity in her gaze. Even bruised, he'd never seen her look more beautiful. He'd never seen anyone look more beautiful.

But she wasn't going to like what he was about to say. He'd never told her about his friendship with the Chase family, but there was no time like the present to come clean.

"You'd better sit."

He patted the sofa cushion next to him, but Kerri dropped into a chair instead, her message very clear. They might have made love last night, but this morning, she was all business.

"Why do I get the feeling I'm not going to be happy about whatever this is?" Her gaze narrowed.

Wade shook his head. "Because you're not."

Her gaze narrowed and she frowned. "Go on."

"McCann thinks Michael Chase is involved in all this."

The color drained from her cheeks. "The mob?"

Wade flinched. He'd always hated that term.

"Not the family. Just the son. Word is he's turned against the family and taken up with Project Liberation."

Kerri's features twisted with confusion. "Why?"

Wade stood and paced to the window, pulling back the curtain and staring at the ocean waves as they pounded the sand.

"That's what I intend to find out."

A moment of silence beat between them.

"What on earth are you talking about?" Kerri's tone dripped with her disbelief.

"I know him." Wade spoke flatly, continuing his scrutiny of the beach. "Michael Chase."

"You lost me."

He turned, knowing what he was about to say wasn't going to do a thing for Kerri's trust quotient.

"We grew up together. He used to be like a brother to me."

Kerri's vivid eyes grew huge. "Are you involved in organized crime? Is that why Pine Ridge was torched?"

Her words hit him like a slap across the face. He'd expected her to be shocked. What he hadn't expected was for her to jump to the worst possible conclusion in the blink of an eye.

"Do you honestly think I'd be involved in organized crime?"

Kerri shrugged. "I'd like to think not, but the truth is, I don't know you anymore, Wade. I haven't known you for a long time."

He glared at her, stunned by her harsh words. "What about last night?"

She said nothing, sitting instead in silence.

Wade crossed to her chair and squatted in front of her, cupping her chin in his fingers. She straightened, moving out of his reach.

"Last night was wonderful," she spoke softly, her voice barely audible. "But my first concern is Tom. If you're involved in organized crime, then I'd like you to leave. Now."

Wade stood, letting her words sink in. So she'd toss him out of their lives just like that, not that he should be surprised. That's exactly what she'd done after John's death.

Wade had lost his best friend and his best friend's family in one fell swoop.

He couldn't blame Kerri for wanting to do whatever it might take to keep Tom safe, but was he prepared to never see them again?

He had to know what was going on. Had to take the meeting. Without it, he was operating on blind faith that McCann's words were true.

He'd have to risk Kerri following through on her threat, and hope like hell she didn't.

"I'm not involved, but I am going to go see him."

"Why?"

"Because if he's involved, he can call off whoever it is that's after Tom. We'll come to some sort of agreement." He paced to one end of the small living room and back. "If he's not involved, he'll be able to find out who is."

Kerri stood, blocking his path. "I won't involve my son with mobsters."

"What if it could save his life?"

She paled again, her features falling slack.

Wade dug into his duffel bag for a clean shirt, then stepped into his boots. "I'm not sure how long this will take. Keep the door locked and don't go anywhere."

"So you're just going to leave?" Kerri gestured angrily. "Bark out orders and leave. Just like that?"

He closed the space between them, gripping her shoulders and pulling her close. "I'm trying to stop whoever's after Tom, can't you see that?"

She swallowed, her eyes bright with anger. Wade lowered his mouth to hers but she backed away, breaking free of his touch.

Disappointment whispered through him, but he shoved it away. He didn't have time to worry about his feelings right now.

He headed for the door, plucking Kerri's keys from the coffee table. "I'll be back as soon as I can."

"I'm not sure we'll be here when you do get back."

Her words stopped him in his tracks, the door to the efficiency partially open.

He pivoted, delivering a look he hoped conveyed the seriousness of what he was about to say.

"You're a smart woman, Red. You know as well as I do that leaving here would be the worst mistake you could make. You two won't make it alone." He jangled her keys in the air. "Plus, I'm taking your car. Just sit tight."

He locked the door and pulled it shut behind him. As he walked toward Kerri's car he shot up a silent prayer that the woman thought with her head and not her temper.

If she and Tom set out by themselves, there'd be no telling what might happen.

The only way Wade could protect them was to stay close at all times, but his gut told him he had to search out Michael Chase. The man just might give them the break they needed to put a stop to the hit on Tom.

As he pulled out of the parking lot, he stole one last look at the efficiency's door.

He was trusting Kerri to stay put. He had no other choice. He certainly couldn't risk taking them with him just in case Chase was involved.

He could only hope they'd be here when he returned.

KERRI SAT AND STARED at the closed door for what seemed like hours after Wade left. She couldn't believe he knew Michael Chase, let alone like a brother.

She'd no sooner decided to open her heart to the man than he'd given her a reason to shut down any emotions she felt for him.

Disappointment and shock tangled inside her.

Organized crime?

The Chase family?

She'd never suspected a connection. Never. Not in all the time she'd known him.

Maybe he had hired someone to torch Pine Ridge for the insurance money. Wasn't that what mobsters did?

She squeezed her eyes shut and blew out a breath. Had he pulled Tom into this mess as part of a plot to clear his name? After all, she knew how important his damned reputation was to him.

She rocked back in the chair and sighed.

What a fool she was. What a weak fool.

She straightened, drawing in a deep breath. It was better Wade dropped this bombshell now than after she'd let him even deeper into her heart, and their lives.

If his involvement with the Chase family had anything to do with the threats to Tom's life she'd... well...she'd... She wasn't sure.

But she knew there'd be no letting him back into their home. She couldn't afford to flirt with the type of danger the Chase family represented.

She scrubbed a hand across her tired face and

winced. Her cheek throbbed from yesterday's attack. She'd searched the efficiency for some kind of over-the-counter pain relief tablets, but had found none.

The bedroom door creaked open and Tom emerged, sleepy-eyed and messy-haired, headed straight for the refrigerator.

She stood and reached out for him, pulling him into a hug.

Fear teased at her, threatening to overcome her senses. If anything happened to her son, she wouldn't be able to go on. She shoved the thought away, unwilling to consider the possibility.

"We don't have any milk, honey. Sorry."

He frowned and tipped his head, eyeing the rumpled blanket on the sofa. "Didn't you sleep last night? You never came to bed."

A guilty warmth heated Kerri's face. She shook her head. "Wade and I…had a lot to talk about."

"Where is he?"

"He had to go take care of something."

Tom shrugged. If only accepting simple answers was as easy for her to do as it was for her nine-year-old.

"What am I supposed to eat?" he asked.

Kerri bit her lip. What was he supposed to eat? She'd brought cereal, but no milk. Pancake mix, but no syrup. No butter.

She eyed her son carefully, amazed at how much changing his hair color had altered his appearance.

As if his thoughts had taken the same path, he grinned. "You look really weird, Mom."

Kerri fingered her now-short hair. "You like it?"

Tom wrinkled his nose. "I don't think so."

She laughed. Out of the mouths of babes. At least the kid was honest. "Me, either."

She studied him for another moment, glanced at the refrigerator and the box of cereal she'd placed on the counter, and made a snap decision.

"We're going out for breakfast." She pushed herself up out of the chair she'd been curled into since the moment Wade left. "Get dressed."

Tom's eyes lit up. "Can we walk on the boardwalk?"

Could they?

Wade's warning echoed through her brain. Maybe she and Tom should sit tight, biding their time in the small, dingy efficiency while the sunshine and boardwalk beckoned them outside.

Kerri moved in front of the mirror, studying herself. Shock filtered through her at how different she looked with short, dark hair. No one would ever recognize her.

She turned to study her son. And they'd be hard-pressed to recognize Tom.

She ruffled his hair and winked. "You bet."

WADE SCANNED BOTH seating areas of the diner as he pushed through the entrance, taking a visual inventory before he made a move toward Michael Chase's table.

He'd called his old friend on his way up the Garden

State Parkway, alluding to McCann's accusation. Michael had agreed to meet for breakfast without hesitation.

Most every booth in the popular diner was occupied. Not uncommon for the middle of the breakfast rush, especially on a Saturday morning. One table in particular piqued Wade's interest.

Two overdressed men sat looking a bit uncomfortable, nursing nothing more than matching mugs of coffee. Taking in their bulk, he had to wonder how they'd even fit between the bench seats and the table.

Michael's bodyguards, no doubt. He spotted Michael just a few booths away and realized he had to be correct—his friend had brought backup. As if Wade would ever present a threat to the man.

Michael raised a hand in greeting and Wade returned the gesture with a nod, making his move toward the booth. He slid into the opposite side, planting himself in the middle of the bench seat.

Michael hadn't changed much since their younger days. Handsome. Well-dressed. Closely cropped brown waves. Hazel eyes glittering with mischief. He'd always been a big guy, probably six-four, if Wade remembered correctly, and he'd never hesitated to utilize his size to intimidate.

He'd been a great friend once upon a time—loyal and protective—but now Wade couldn't be sure whether he should consider Michael a friend or foe.

"Want to tell me what you were talking about when

you called?" Michael asked, his expression controlled and unemotional.

A waitress slowed long enough to ask if Wade wanted coffee, then continued past.

Wade leaned forward, dropping his voice. "Someone torched my site. You hear about that?"

Michael nodded. "You don't think I had anything to do with that, do you?"

Wade shrugged. "Local Homeland Security office says you're in bed with Project Liberation."

"Those save-the-trees people?" Michael tipped back his head and laughed, amusement dancing in his eyes. "You're kidding me, right? How long have you known me?"

"Long time."

Michael nodded. "And don't you think I'd rather put up a parking lot and make money any day over saving some trees?"

Wade dropped his voice lower still. "Word is you've turned against the family." He arched one eyebrow. "Maybe Project Liberation has something you need."

Michael's expression morphed from amused to threatening. "I would never turn against the family. Got it?"

Wade nodded, pursing his lips. The waitress reappeared with his coffee and topped off Michael's mug while she was at the table. Neither man said a word until she was out of range.

Wade lowered his voice. "Do I have your word you're not involved with Project Liberation?"

Michael's mouth drew up into a crooked grin. "Maybe you should worry about who torched Pine Ridge and leave family business to me and Dad."

Wade's pulse quickened. "So you are involved?"

Michael sat back, crossing his arms over his chest. "I told you. Why the hell would I be involved with a bunch of tree-huggers?"

"I've been thinking about that the whole way here. The only thing I can come up with is to sabotage another family's construction sites, but it seems to me anything that's happened recently has been at a Chase site."

One dark eyebrow lifted tauntingly. "Until Pine Ridge." A slow smile spread across Michael's lips. "You think people don't know the old man got you started?"

Wade winced inwardly. Vincent Chase had provided the start-up money for Sorenson Construction years earlier. Wade had repaid the loan in full, but had always been afraid the connection would come back to haunt him—and his reputation.

"I need you to come clean on this one," Wade said flatly.

Michael's features tensed, leaving no room for misunderstanding how serious he was. "And I need you to mind your own business. This doesn't concern you. If you know what's good for you, you'll drop this."

"Drop this?" Wade's voice climbed in intensity. "How am I supposed to drop this when there have been two attempts on the life of the witness I convinced to come forward?"

"Always did have a knack for jumping in where you didn't belong."

"The boy's mother was attacked. These people committed murder. Don't you think they'll stop at nothing until they've silenced Tom? Tell me where to find them."

Michael's lips twisted into a wry grin. "So you can do what? Ride in on your white stallion and place them under citizen's arrest?"

Wade leaned across the table, more than infuriated by Michael's tone. The man's henchmen both stood up, bumping against the table with two loud thuds.

Michael held up a hand without glancing in their direction, and they sank back into their respective sides of the booth.

Wade sat back, studying his old friend. "You're pretty calm for a guy the police think turned against the family."

"That's because it's a load of crap." Michael clinked his mug against Wade's in a mock toast.

"So you really don't know what's going on?"

Michael pursed his lips and narrowed his gaze. "Would I tell you if I did? You're my friend, Wade, I don't want to see you get hurt." He leaned forward. "These Project Liberation bastards are everywhere. You can't handle this on your own."

"Who says I'm on my own?"

Michael laughed. "I grew up with you, remember? I know you."

"Fair enough."

"You'll take the protection?"

Wade shook his head. "No. I just wanted to see your face when I asked if you were involved."

Michael's features fell serious, intense. "And the verdict?"

Wade studied his old friend. "I think you're just as good at keeping secrets as you ever were."

He shrugged. "You need to trust the family."

Wade tossed some bills on the table and eased out of the booth. "Thanks, but no thanks."

Michael slid the money back toward Wade. "I've got this covered." He nailed Wade with a look that stopped him in his tracks. "No one will know you and I met, but I think you should talk to the old man."

Wade shook his head.

Michael's eyebrows lifted. "Do you want to keep this kid alive or don't you?"

"Yes, but I don't want to—"

Michael held up a hand. "You won't owe anyone. You repaid your debt to my dad a long time ago. You'll stay in the clear, you don't have to worry."

"I'm not—"

"I know what makes you tick," Michael interrupted. "Your saintly reputation. But there's more to this situation than you can possibly imagine."

"Like what?"

"Let's just say the interested parties have formed an alliance to take down the Chase family."

The puzzle pieces floating through Wade's mind

became more and more murky. "Why do the police think you're involved?"

Michael shrugged with his eyes. "Let them think what they want. I'm clean." He tipped his cup toward Wade. "You, however, have a decision to make."

Wade pondered Michael's words for several moments. He'd vowed years before to steer clear of any involvement with the Chase family. Once he'd repaid his loan, he'd been free of all ties—all links.

Was he willing to toss that aside, simply to ask for protection?

If push came to shove, yes. Kerri and Tom's lives were worth any price.

He pushed up and away from the table, this time turning toward the door. "I'll think about it."

"Better think quickly," Michael's voice trailed after him. "After all, the third time's the charm."

The words crashed against the edge of Wade's remaining doubt. He'd failed Tom so far. Yes, the boy was still alive, but the two attempts had been too close, and they never should have happened.

Fate may have finally brought Wade's past crashing into his present. After all these years, the Chase family might be the only way out for Tom and Kerri.

Michael's voice pounded at his brain.

Third time's the charm.

Not if Wade had anything to say about it.

He gunned Kerri's car out of the lot and headed back toward Wildwood.

The third time might be the charm, but he planned to do everything in his power to make sure the third time never happened.

Chapter Nine

Kerri watched as Tom racked up yet more prize tickets at the skee-ball machine. The kid was amazing. She'd never been very good at rolling the wooden balls into anything but the lowest slot, but Tom was the master. It was as if he'd been born to hurl the balls through the fifty-point slot every time.

He looked back at her and held up a finger, asking the question with his eyes.

"One more game," she answered. "I'll wait outside."

She'd eaten so many pancakes at breakfast she needed the salt air to keep her awake, though at the moment she'd like nothing better than to head back to the efficiency and take a nap.

Her face had begun to throb, but she'd located a pair of large sunglasses and some aspirin at one of the boardwalk variety stores. She hadn't drawn any stares since, so she figured the glasses must have hidden most of her bruising.

She sank onto one of the benches outside the arcade

and wrapped her arms around herself, thinking about last night's lovemaking, much as she'd tried to block all thoughts of Wade from her mind.

She ached this morning in all the right places. Her marriage to John had grown so distant and cold before his death she honestly couldn't remember how many years it had been since she'd made love. And she'd never made love to anyone with the passion she'd felt for Wade last night.

Kerri shot a glance at Tom, wondering if he'd done as she'd asked or whether he'd sneaked in a second extra game.

Thankfully, he'd slept straight through the night. She and Wade had made every effort to be quiet, although that had proved next to impossible in the small space.

As she watched Tom roll yet another fifty-point ball, she had the sensation of being watched and turned slightly to look over her shoulder.

Wasn't that the same man who'd been sitting outside the pancake house earlier?

She kept a casual eye on the man, not wanting him to catch her staring. Could he be following them? Could he be the man from Pine Ridge? Or the van? Or the cabin?

Her stomach tightened, fear taking hold and squeezing at her insides.

The man was wearing a ball cap, making it all the more difficult to see his features. Kerri took a deep breath and held it. Her imagination might be working overtime, but her instincts told her otherwise.

Tom appeared by her side a few moments later, and she stood, linking her arm through his and hurrying him away from the arcade.

"Mom."

"We'll come back later." She lied, having no intention of bringing her son out in the open again.

She'd been an idiot to bring Tom out to breakfast—out on the boardwalk, for heaven's sake. So what if she was so angry with Wade she could spit? That was no reason to take chances—foolish chances.

"Mom." Tom stopped dead in his tracks. "Bumper cars. You promised."

Kerri looked down into her son's pale eyes and weakened. She didn't want to alarm him when she might be imagining things.

She glanced behind them, scanning the relatively light crowd of tourists. The sun beat down brightly from above, casting a glare even through her sunglasses. Kerri shielded her face with her hand. Her gaze landed on a man sitting on the bench, reading the paper.

Not the same man. Different cap.

She breathed a sigh of relief, but then spotted a second man leaning against the railing.

No. Still someone else. The other man had been heavier. Taller.

"Mom?"

Tom's pleading tone jerked her focus away from her frenzied scan of the crowd.

"Okay," she said reluctantly. "One ride." She pulled

the tickets from her pocket and tore off the number indicated on the ride's sign. "Make it quick."

Tom raced up the ramp, practically vibrating inside his skin as he waited for the attendant to let him through.

She hadn't seen her son this excited since... Her heart ached. Since his father had died. They hadn't taken a family vacation after the summer before that, and they hadn't been to Wildwood since Tom was barely more than a toddler.

Tom waved as he climbed into a car, and Kerri waved back, moving along the railing to get a clear view of the track.

The majority of the cars were empty this early in the day. The beach beyond the boardwalk swarmed with vacationers who would no doubt fill the amusement pier later that night, but for now, she and Tom were among the minority who had chosen to walk under the unforgiving midday August sun.

A buzzer rang and the cars jerked into motion. Tom deftly steered and accelerated out onto the track, avoiding the rubber tires on the shoulder as he headed directly for another boy's car.

Bump.

Success. A grin spread wide across Tom's face, and Kerri felt herself begin to relax.

No one knew they were here. She was overreacting to seeing the same man twice. They had nothing to worry about as long as they stayed put and made no outside contact.

She waved to Tom then leaned against the railing, turning her back to the track to take in the view of the ocean.

The man from the pancake house and the arcade sat on a bench directly opposite from where she stood.

Her heart caught in her throat and her stomach did a slow sideways roll.

Damn.

Two sightings she could write off to coincidence. Three was one too many.

The man met her gaze and smiled. A tight, bone-chilling smile.

Kerri looked away quickly, glancing back toward the track.

Tom's car continued to careen from car to car, moving now in the middle of a pack of vehicles.

She had to get him out of there and off this boardwalk. They had to somehow lose this guy and get back to the efficiency.

She glanced back to where the man had been sitting, but he'd vanished, leaving his newspaper behind.

A chill raced down her spine just as the buzzer on the bumper car ride sounded.

Ride over.

Thank God.

When Tom bounded to her side, chattering away about his strategy and successes, she merely grabbed his hand and steered him toward the bench, instinctively needing to see whatever it was the man had been reading.

As she neared, the newspaper's banner came into focus. *Pocono Record.*

Her pulse quickened and she squinted, struggling to locate the paper's date of issue.

August 18.

Yesterday.

Kerri's mouth went dry and her surroundings did a quick spin.

I'm going to do everything in my power to keep my son's location a secret.

Her words to Wade echoed through her mind.

What a fool she'd been to bring Tom out into the open. Someone knew exactly where they were and exactly what they looked like—altered appearances and all.

There was only one thing to do.

Run.

WADE'S HEART STUTTERED to a stop when he pulled Kerri's car back into the boardwalk efficiency's parking lot. The door to number 202, their room, sat ajar. But why?

Dread pooled in his gut. He launched himself from the driver's seat and sprinted toward the steps, taking them two at a time until he hit the landing. He was at the efficiency door in three strides.

He hesitated, pressing himself to the wall outside the door, listening for noise, voices, anything.

He heard nothing.

Wade turned, pushing the door open with his toe.

His gut caught and twisted.

The outer living area had been tossed, the sofa's cushions slashed, foam stuffing scattered across the floor. The small kitchen area had been upended, drawers and utensils, bowls and plates, food items lay strewn over every inch of the faded linoleum floor.

"Kerri! Tom!"

Nothing.

He scuffled through the mess, making his way toward the bedroom door. He stopped cold when he reached the threshold. What little clothing Kerri and Tom had brought with them had been tossed about the room, the drawers of the small wicker clothing chest pulled from their tracks and discarded haphazardly wherever they had landed.

Tom's beloved sleeping bag had been sliced into shreds. The blinds had been partially pulled off the window and sunbeams cast a bright pattern across the chaotic scene.

As Tom pulled his cell phone from his pocket, something on the cheap carpet glimmered. His breath caught.

Kerri's amethyst heart.

If she and Tom had left as she threatened, would she have left the stone behind? He crossed to where it sat and bent down, gripping the heavy object in his hand. He stood, giving the heart a bounce on his palm.

Who was he kidding? Any idiot could take one look at this room and know Kerri and Tom hadn't left of their own free will. But why were there no police? No hotel management? Surely damage of this magnitude would have made a hell of a lot of noise.

The crash of the surf sounded from outside and tourists' voices filled the air. Wade stepped back to the front door, staring—stunned—at the beach as he punched McCann's number on his cell.

He'd always heard daytime robberies were a piece of cake during the summer in shore communities. The tourists spent the day on the beach, and surely the rooms in this hotel were filled with nothing but tourists, with the exception of number 202.

"McCann."

"You'd better get to Wildwood, and call in the local authorities."

Wade's tone had gone flat, intent. Fury began to boil inside him. He'd strangle whoever had done this, if he could. If someone had harmed so much as one hair on Kerri or Tom's head, there'd be hell to pay.

The bottom fell out of Wade's stomach as he looked back at the scene of destruction.

He'd screwed up leaving them alone. But how had someone found them? And so fast?

They must have been followed. All of his precautions and back road driving hadn't done one bit of good. He'd made a promise to Kerri and Tom and he'd blown it.

Third time's the charm.

Chase's words haunted him.

"What in the hell happened?" McCann snarled across the line.

As Wade filled him in, he could only hope Kerri and Tom hadn't paid for his mistake with their lives.

PLEASURE FLOODED through him at the blatant fear painted across the mother's face when she saw the paper. He had to admit, leaving it on the bench had been a nice touch. A message, if ever there was one.

He knew the ball cap covered most of his features, yet he'd feared the kid might recognize him. He should have known the boy would be so wrapped up in the excitement of the boardwalk he wouldn't give him a second glance.

He figured the mother hadn't had much of a chance to see his face yesterday, but he couldn't be sure.

He rubbed the knuckles of his hand. The small cuts and bruising left behind by his punches caused stabs of pain when touched. He found the sensation oddly satisfying.

Another addition to the list of things that brought him pleasure.

His talents as a fire-starter had been well appreciated by a variety of organizations, but perhaps he'd been missing out on a whole other area of freelance work.

He could have been a thug.

He laughed out loud, then caught himself, once again going silent, stepping back into the side alley between the bumper car ride and a discount jewelry store.

He already knew where the mother and the boy were staying, so following them wasn't a necessity. He'd arranged for an associate to pay a visit while they were out.

As far as he was concerned, he'd rather hit them while they were on the run, which his associate's handiwork would no doubt ensure.

He stepped out of the shadows as the mother and son hurried away, being careful to stay out of her field of vision as she glanced around the boardwalk.

He had to admit he admired the woman's attempt to change their appearances, but her efforts were nothing but predictable. She should have known that.

She was attractive no matter what. Not many women could say that. The boy was attractive, too. A good-looking kid.

Too bad he wouldn't live long enough to become a good-looking man.

Chapter Ten

Kerri gripped Tom's hand tightly in hers and hurried him along the boardwalk, glancing to her left and her right nervously.

"Mom. What's wrong with you?" Tom's voice sounded tighter than normal, full of worry.

Kerri winced. Her son was too young to be faced with the danger Wade's determination had thrust upon them.

"I think we need to get back." She worked to keep her tone light, but failed miserably. "Wade will be worried if we're not there when he gets back from his errands."

She hadn't told Tom where Wade had gone. That would have been insane. Instead, she'd simply said he'd gone out for supplies and food.

Tom looked up at her, his eyebrows furrowed. "You think the man that's after us will find us?"

Kerri's stomach flipped. She hated for Tom to be exposed to all of this. He'd been through too much already in his young life.

No one should lose their father at age six, and no one

should witness a violent crime just a few years later, but he had. And now they'd deal with it. Together.

She decided to tell the truth. "I think I saw someone, honey. We need to get off the boardwalk."

Tom's eyes grew huge. "Here?"

If she wasn't mistaken, excitement gleamed in his pale gaze.

"This isn't one of your mystery books, Tom. This is real life." She quickened her pace, knowing her son would have no trouble keeping up.

Kerri turned toward a side street, taking the boardwalk ramp down to the sidewalk. Older condos and hotels lined the street, their pastel paint faded and chipped from years of exposure to the sun and salt air.

Wildwood had once been the place to be along the southern coast of New Jersey, then parts of the town had fallen into decay. Revitalization plans were under way, but as Kerri glanced up and down the block, she wasn't sure the efforts had reached this particular section.

She hesitated, not sure whether or not to head out to the main drag.

"We should cut between houses, Mom." Tom's tone had brightened. As much as she didn't want him thinking this was some sort of game, she'd rather hear excitement than fear in his voice.

"Good thinking."

She kept a firm grip on his hand and headed to her left, turning south toward their hotel efficiency. If she'd been accurate in keeping track of blocks, they had seven to cover before they ran into their building.

Surely they could evade the guy in the ball cap, and she prayed Wade would be back by the time they returned. As much as she wanted to throttle him for putting them in this position with his infuriating need to put his reputation above all else, she needed him now. Tom needed him.

Wade had been right. She couldn't protect Tom by herself, and as much as she hated to admit any sort of weakness, she wouldn't let pride keep her from letting Wade protect her son.

They dashed between houses, across concrete driveways and up sandy side yards. Dogs barked. Car doors slammed. Every sharp noise sent Kerri's nerves screaming to attention, but she never spotted the man again.

No ball cap.

No shadows.

Maybe she'd imagined the whole thing. Maybe the Pocono newspaper had been a coincidence.

She shuddered as their hotel came into sight. Two police cars sat at odd angles in the parking lot, their red-and-blue light bars flashing like strobes. The door to their room sat wide open and the flurry of activity inside was evident.

The newspaper had been no coincidence. Something had gone wrong.

"Mom." Tom's voice was barely more than a whisper.

She stopped in her tracks, pulling him behind her protectively.

When she spotted the familiar bumper of her car just beyond one of the police cruisers, her mouth went dry.

Wade was back.

But had he returned before whatever had happened to draw the police? Or had he stumbled upon something in their efficiency?

She took a backward step, taking Tom with her.

Kerri had no intention of walking into a situation that might expose her son. Until she saw Wade's face, she couldn't presume it was safe to go back.

She pulled Tom close to the side of the building across the street from their hotel, intent on waiting and watching until she could put together the pieces of whatever had happened.

She tucked her son tightly against her side, shielding him from the view of anyone who might look out of the second-floor room.

"What are we going to do, Mom?" he whispered.

"We're going to wait right here."

"But what about Wade?" Tom's voice cracked on Wade's name and Kerri knew he was frightened. "What if something happened to him?"

Kerri drew in a deep breath. "I'm sure he's fine."

But she had no way of knowing that. What if something *had* happened to Wade? Fear teased at her insides.

She and Tom would have to disappear. She wasn't sure where they'd go or how they'd get there, but she was sure of one thing. She'd find a way. And she wouldn't trust the police to protect them. Look how well they'd done so far.

No. She and Tom would have to make their way alone. Lord knew they'd done it before. They could do it again.

No matter what it took.

Maybe once McCann and the police had the guilty parties behind bars, she and Tom could come back. But as things stood now, she'd rather build a new life from scratch than risk her son's safety in order to return to her old life.

Tom was all she had left. And she had no intention of letting anything happen to him.

WADE STOOD BACK as the responding officers picked through the scene. It had taken them close to forty-five minutes to arrive. Forty-five minutes of God knew what that might be happening to Kerri and Tom.

He never should have listened to McCann. Shouldn't have waited. He should have gone out on his own, searching for them.

Reality settled into his bones.

Who was he kidding? He had no idea of where to start looking. Unless Kerri and Tom had made an escape. Maybe they'd gotten away, headed toward the crowds on the beach, or the boardwalk.

When McCann's cruiser pulled into the lot, Wade breathed a sigh of relief. He had confidence in his old friend, unlike what he felt toward these guys.

McCann was alone when he climbed out of the car, his face drawn with lines of fatigue, or frustration—

Wade couldn't tell which. He tipped his chin in Wade's direction as he cleared the top of the steps, but checked in with the officers on the scene before he did anything else.

After a few minutes, he headed toward Wade, shoving a hand through his hair as he walked. "Hell of a mess."

Wade gave a tight nod. "No kidding."

"I told you to let me handle your relocation, but you had to go off on your own."

Wade winced. "You're not saying anything I haven't been saying to myself since I found the room like this."

"Any idea of where the kid and his mother are?" McCann widened his eyes expectantly.

Confusion whirled in the pit of Wade's stomach. "That's why I called you."

McCann shook his head. "There's no sign of struggle."

Wade couldn't believe what he was hearing. He gestured toward the open door and the destruction inside. "What do you call that?"

"A lot of show. Deliberate damage." He lowered his voice. "A warning. These guys aren't playing around. You've got to let me get that kid to a safe house."

Wade paced away from McCann then pivoted on one heel, retracing his steps. Anger surged inside him and he did nothing to hide the emotion.

"What about you catching whoever did this? Whoever set that fire?" He stepped toe to toe with McCann. "How about that?"

McCann didn't flinch. Didn't step back. Held his ground. "I told you about the Michael Chase connection. We're working it."

"He's got nothing to do with it," Wade said.

McCann narrowed his gaze. "How would you know?"

"Because I went to see him."

Now it was McCann's turn to turn away angrily. "You went to see a suspect in the middle of my investigation? What are you trying to do? Get the kid killed?" He pointed back at the upended efficiency. "Did you tell him where you were staying?"

Wade shook his head. "He didn't do this. He wouldn't."

McCann leaned close. "Oh, and you're the expert, I suppose."

Wade nodded. "In this case, I am."

They stood in silence for several awkward moments.

Wade broke the silence. "What are you going to do to find Kerri and Tom?"

"Wait for them to come back. Then I'm going to move them to a safe house. Far from Wildwood."

Wade opened his mouth to protest, but McCann held up a hand to cut him off.

"This time you don't have a say. This is my case. My witness. He goes where I say he goes. Understood?"

But Wade didn't agree verbally or nonverbally.

"What makes you so sure they're coming back?" he asked.

McCann jerked a thumb toward the hotel office. "Manager told one of the officers he saw a woman and her kid headed toward the boardwalk a few hours ago. Description fit except for the hair. I'm assuming they colored it? Cut it?"

Wade nodded.

"Original."

McCann's know-it-all attitude pushed Wade's anger close to the edge, but he held it together. McCann was right. They were amateurs. *He* was an amateur.

What had he been thinking when he decided he could keep Kerri and Tom safe on his own?

And the boardwalk? Why would Kerri risk taking Tom there? Unless she'd felt safe enough—or been angry enough—to make a rash decision.

He walked to the railing and drew in a deep breath of salt air. When he turned back to ask McCann if they shouldn't search the boardwalk, his gaze hit and held on something odd.

Two pairs of feet extended beyond the side of the building across the street, as if two people had sat down to wait for something or someone, backs propped against the wall.

On a hunch, he headed toward the steps. "I'll be right back."

"Where are you going?" McCann's tone had gone thick with annoyance.

Wade never answered, focused instead on the building across the street, praying fervently his hunch was right and Kerri and Tom were safe and sound, laying low until they knew it was safe to return.

AN ANXIOUS DREAD squeezed at Kerri's throat when she heard the approaching footsteps. She tightened her grip on Tom's hand, who responded by leaning around the corner to peek, exactly as she'd asked him not to.

"Uncle Wade." His voice sang out and he slipped his hand from hers, launching himself at the man who now stood towering over them both.

She let her gaze wander from Wade's boots to the jeans she'd watched him strip out of the night before, to his clean T-shirt, to the frown on his handsome face.

He looked tired. More tired than she'd ever seen him before. Even more tired than he'd appeared in the days following John's death. Lines of worry creased his forehead and pulled at the corners of his mouth.

"What happened?" she asked softly.

"I could ask you the same thing." His expression didn't soften. If anything, it grew more intent.

"We went out to breakfast." She spoke the words flatly, knowing how foolish she sounded. How foolish she'd been. "I think we were followed."

"Uncle Wade, you should have seen it." Tom's voice jumped two octaves in his excitement. "There was a man in a cap and Mom saw him outside the pancake house and the arcade and the bumper cars."

When Wade looked at Kerri she caught a tangle of anger and concern in his eyes.

"He left a paper, and you'll never believe it," Tom continued. "It was from yesterday and from the

Poconos." He fisted his small hands on his hips. "He followed us."

Wade sank to his haunches, squatting in front of Kerri. "Did you get a good look at his face?"

She shook her head. "He had on a ball cap. But it was the same guy in three places."

"With a Pocono newspaper?"

She swallowed down the tightness that had settled in her throat. "The *Pocono Record.* Yesterday's issue."

"He didn't follow you back here?"

She shook her head again.

"We were careful," Tom interjected. "Stayed in the alleys and everything."

Kerri took a deep breath then sighed. "I'm sorry. I screwed up."

Wade straightened, reaching into the front pocket of his jeans. When he held out his hand, Kerri's amethyst heart sat squarely in his palm. "You forgot this."

He handed her the stone, studying her face intently.

Kerri dropped her focus to the heart then redirected her attention to Wade. "I didn't forget it. I was coming back."

He nodded. "Fair enough."

She climbed to her feet, brushing sand off her shorts. "What happened?" She tipped her chin toward the hotel.

"The room got tossed." Wade turned and stood next to her.

"Bad?" Her belly tightened.

"Very."

Silence beat between them for several long seconds.

"McCann's inside." Wade's upbeat tone sounded forced. "He wants to move us to a safe house away from here."

Kerri turned to look at Wade, her eyes searching his face. "Do you trust him?"

He nodded, then stole a glance at Tom, who stood with his back to them, intently watching the police activity across the street.

"But the last time he placed us, they found us the same day."

"We'll make sure that doesn't happen again." He held out his hand to her. "It'll be just the four of us when we make that decision."

"Then, let's go," Kerri said, slipping her fingers into Wade's hand. The firm contact bolstered her resolve. She wanted Wade near. Chase family contacts or not.

She could only pray she was making the right choice.

Her son's life depended on it.

Chapter Eleven

The police were clearing out as Wade led Kerri and Tom back to the room.

McCann stood waiting inside, tapping his foot impatiently. "You just had to do things your way, didn't you?"

"We've covered this already." Wade cut his eyes toward Kerri and Tom, hoping McCann would get the message to cool it.

If anything, the move had the opposite effect.

Kerri and Tom stood together in the doorway, visibly shaken by the sight of the damage inside. McCann walked toward them, not stepping around a thing, but rather stomping across cereal, sofa stuffing and silverware.

McCann's toe clipped a spoon and sent it flying.

Wade winced at the racket.

When the detective leaned close to Kerri's face, Wade stepped between them, pressing a palm to McCann's chest, pushing him back two steps.

"What were you thinking? Taking a stroll?" McCann's face flushed red with anger.

Kerri pulled herself taller, her eyes narrowing on the man as she tugged Tom behind her. Like a momma bear protecting her cub.

Wade couldn't remember when—if ever—he'd seen such intensity flash in her eyes.

"For your information, Detective McCann, we went out to eat because we had to travel without much in the way of preparation time."

She held up one finger. "The first time after someone tried to run my son down."

Another finger. "The second time after the cabin you recommended was found almost immediately by whoever is after my son."

Wade searched McCann's face for any sign of softening, but saw none. The man's features remained firm.

"You could have been spotted." McCann spoke the words slowly and deliberately.

The group stood in silence for a moment then Wade and Kerri exchanged a quick glance.

McCann let out a short burst of breath and shoved a hand up through his hair. "Don't tell me. You've been seen?"

"Maybe," Wade interrupted.

McCann held up a hand to stop Wade from speaking. Wade resisted the instinct to shove it away.

"Tell me." McCann looked nowhere but directly into Kerri's face.

Kerri detailed what had happened—step by step—

right down to their trek home from the boardwalk, up side alleys and between buildings.

McCann moved past Kerri and Tom and stepped out onto the balcony, scanning the parking lot below and the area across the street.

When he turned around, his eyes shone with determination. "We've got to move you now." He shook his head. "No picking through your belongings, no nothing." He jerked a thumb toward the door. "We just go."

"Where?" Kerri said softly.

"I'm thinking on that." McCann reentered the efficiency and paced a tight pattern through the debris. "I'm thinking."

Empathy eased through Wade as he watched Kerri ruffle Tom's hair. The kid was pale, visibly tired and scared. He probably wanted nothing more than to retrieve his books and his video games and go home.

Wade couldn't help him with the latter right now, but he could with the former.

"McCann." Wade spoke the name sharply.

His old friend stopped in his tracks and spun to face him, his expression expectant.

Wade tipped his head toward the bedroom. "Why don't you let them look while you think?"

McCann twisted up his mouth, as if Wade's sentimentality annoyed him, but he nodded just the same. "Make it quick."

"I have a client I need to call," Kerri said softly as she brushed past Wade. "I've got to find my address book."

"No." McCann reached out for her, gripping her upper arm. "You can't call anyone, understood?"

Kerri blinked. "But this couple commissioned a sculpture for a special event. I've got to tell them I won't be delivering the piece."

"They'll figure that out when you don't show up." McCann thinned his lips. "I know this is tough, but as far as the outside world is concerned, you and Tom are gone." He snapped his fingers. "Into thin air. Understood?"

Kerri showed no response other than drawing in a deep breath.

"Forever?" Tom's voice had gone soft, sad.

The detective turned to look at him, studying him for a moment. "Just until the trial."

"But you haven't even caught anyone," Kerri said.

"We will." McCann released her arm and resumed his pacing. "We will."

KERRI COULDN'T BELIEVE the state of the bedroom when she stepped through the door.

Tom had gone in ahead of her and now sat on the floor, eyes swimming with tears as he cradled the remains of his beloved books in his lap.

"We'll replace them." Kerri spoke gently, realizing the promise did little to soothe her son's wounded spirit.

She could only hope that with time this entire nightmare would become a distant memory in Tom's mind.

Her son deserved to be home skateboarding with

buddies, sneaking into the woods to read a book, lying on the sidewalk staring up at the clouds.

He deserved to be a nine-year-old.

He didn't deserve to be the sole witness to a violent crime. A witness on the run, yanked out of the life he'd known.

Kerri moved to where Tom sat and sank to the floor next to him. She tipped his chin to study his face, brushing back a lock of his darkened hair.

"I'm sorry, honey."

He looked up from the broken book spines and shredded pages and forced a smile, a glimmer of strength reigniting in the depths of his pale eyes.

"It's all right, Mom. We're doing the right thing." He nodded. "We're going to get the bad guys and put them away for good."

Kerri smiled and pressed a kiss to his forehead. "I'm proud of you."

She couldn't bring herself to agree with him. Matter of fact, she'd grown to soundly regret ever letting Wade talk Tom into coming forward.

If she and Tom had never said anything, none of this would have happened.

And a widow with three children wouldn't have a chance at justice and closure in the murder of her husband.

Kerri centered herself and climbed to her feet.

Maybe they were doing the right thing, but heaven help her if she didn't wish things had gone a bit differently.

Understatement of the century.

She moved to the opposite side of the bedroom, casting a glance at Tom's treasured sleeping bag, tattered and in ruins. She toed at the items strewn across the carpet until she spotted what she wanted.

A sliver of burgundy.

Her address book.

She breathed a sigh of relief to find the small booklet intact and slipped it into the back pocket of her shorts without uttering a word.

Detective McCann might not want her to call her client, but Wade Sorenson wasn't the only one who gave a damn about his reputation.

Without her commissioned sculptures, Kerri would have little to no income. John had been light on life insurance, and she and Tom had grown to depend on the money her artwork brought in.

If she failed to deliver this piece, bad word of mouth would spread like wildfire.

She'd never get another referral in the Philadelphia or South Jersey region.

She had to find a way to make the call. She'd be careful, but she *would* make the call.

No matter what McCann dictated.

A SHORT WHILE LATER, Wade headed south on the Garden State Parkway, following McCann's cruiser toward the Cape May to Lewes ferry.

McCann had decided on a safe house in a rural area

of Delaware, just west of the beaches. By taking the ferry, they'd be able to reach Lewes in less than two hours.

According to McCann, the house was an hour's drive beyond that.

Kerri sat quietly in the passenger seat, staring out the window. Tom had managed to find his video game unharmed during his search of the bedroom, and now contentedly worked his levels as he sat in the backseat.

"I know something's eating at you." Wade shot a quick glance in Kerri's direction. "Want to talk about it?"

She turned to face him, disbelief blatant in her eyes. "You mean other than uprooting my child and the two attempts on his life?"

She dropped her voice to a whisper, but Wade had no doubt eagle ears in the backseat had picked up every word. He glanced in the rearview mirror in time to see Tom look up then quickly back down at his game.

Just as Wade had thought.

The kid didn't miss a thing.

Wade refocused on the road, the muscles in his jaw contracting. "Yeah. Other than that."

Kerri leaned toward Wade conspiratorially, but Tom leaned over the back of the seat, bright-eyed and alert, butting his head between them.

Kerri let out a sigh, glared at her son, then spoke. "Why are we blindly following McCann to some un-disclosed location in rural Delaware?"

Wade frowned. "Because it's his job to protect us and

we trust him." He jerked a thumb at Tom. "He's trying to hide your son, remember?"

Kerri raked her fingers through her short hair. "But there's obviously a leak in the department. I don't see how we can trust him, even if he means well."

The skin around her eyes wrinkled with her frown, drawing Wade's attention to the nasty bruising that seemed to have worsened instead of improved.

"He doesn't know how our pursuers found us at the cabin," Kerri continued, holding up her hands. "Who's to say they aren't going to find us now?"

She wasn't saying anything Wade hadn't already considered, but he felt the situation had grown critical enough to follow McCann's lead.

"We should have stayed in Wildwood." Tom's voice interrupted Wade's thoughts.

"Why?" he asked.

"Because the man after us will expect us to leave." Tom shrugged. "Maybe he scared us on purpose just to get us out of Wildwood. Maybe he wanted us to run."

Wade had to give it to the kid. He had a definite point.

He turned to Kerri, letting up on the accelerator to put a little distance between their car and McCann's.

There was an exit coming up, and if they were about to make the decision Wade's gut was urging him to make, he needed to be ready.

Kerri's eyes had gone wide. "Tom makes sense."

"He does," Wade agreed.

He made perfect sense.

McCann had said the destruction at the hotel was a warning. Perhaps it had been done to flush Kerri and Tom out of hiding. They might be doing exactly what their pursuer had wanted them to do.

Somewhere in McCann's department there was a leak. There had to be. Whoever it was had managed to overhear what they'd thought was a private conversation about the cabin. What was to stop that same person from uncovering the location of the house in Delaware?

The sign for the last exit before Cape May appeared along the shoulder. The lines for the exit lane began, widening off to the right.

Wade slowed, easing his foot even farther off the gas pedal. He had to make a decision and he had to make it now.

He glanced once at Kerri, asking her opinion with his eyes.

She gave a single nod.

Wade swerved the car onto the exit ramp at the last second, bumping over the rumble strips. He silently hoped McCann wouldn't miss them for a moment or two, giving Wade just enough time to slip onto the back roads and out of sight.

Once McCann went too far to back up to the exit, he'd have one heck of a time doubling back. Plus, he'd have no idea of which direction Wade had taken.

Wade supposed there was always the possibility McCann could issue an APB on Kerri's car. He negotiated a turn onto a sparsely traveled road, then pressed down on the accelerator. He had to get them back into Wildwood and somehow get the car hidden as quickly as possible.

When Wade's cell phone rang, he pressed the power-off button without looking to see the incoming number.

He knew perfectly well who was calling, but he planned to avoid contact for as long as he could.

As they headed back toward Wildwood, he could only hope he'd made the right decision, and not one that might cost them everything.

Chapter Twelve

Kerri had an odd sense of déjà vu.

She'd just tucked Tom into bed, this time in a rented bungalow close to the Wildwood boardwalk. Wade had stopped at the first real estate office they'd seen and asked for a weekend rental.

The Realtor had been more than happy to accommodate—and take cash. Kerri couldn't help but wonder if the rental would ever show up on the agency books.

She chased the thought out of her head.

Who cared? The honesty of some real estate agent meant nothing in the grand scheme of things. More specifically, in the grand scheme of their lives.

Wade had taken a trip to the corner grocery store and they were stocked with essentials. Milk, bread, eggs, cereal. They might only have the clothes on their back, but at least they wouldn't starve.

As fate would have it, the bungalow offered off-street parking—literally off the street—as in the alley behind the house. She knew it wasn't much, but she and

Wade had agreed that the fact the car wasn't in plain view might help them evade discovery just long enough for him to figure out their next move.

Kerri sank into the sofa, this one a nubby bluish-green tweed. Wade hadn't left the window ever since they'd eaten dinner, and she wanted to talk to him.

No, correct that. She needed to talk to him.

Try as she might to make sense of all that had happened since the day of the Pine Ridge fire, she simply couldn't make the details fit nicely together.

Based on the intent look on Wade's face, he was mulling over the same topic.

"Wade." She patted the sofa cushion next to her, noting the dark stubble that shadowed his lower face. He'd apparently run a hand through his hair, and his T-shirt had come untucked from his jeans.

Her stomach did a sideways tilt, but she did her best to ignore the sensation, not wanting to be distracted by her physical attraction to the man.

"Come talk to me," she said, giving the cushion another pat.

He moved toward her and sat down, legs crossed ankle to knee. "You all right? How's that cheekbone?"

Kerri reached to her face and winced. She hadn't taken anything for the pain since her boardwalk excursion and the throbbing had returned.

"It's not bad." She lied, not wanting Wade to have another thing to worry about.

"You never were a good liar."

Wade patted her knee then stood, heading toward the kitchen. A few moments later he returned holding a few ice cubes wrapped in a paper towel.

"This will no doubt be a case of too little too late, but maybe it'll help some."

He gently held the ice to Kerri's face and she reached to take the paper towel from him.

Wade shook his head. "Let me do this."

"I'm capable of holding ice on my face." Kerri rankled.

Wade grinned. "I never said you weren't. I only said I wanted to do this for you."

His words sent Kerri's insides spiraling into a tight coil of heat. "Thanks."

She sat back against the sofa and closed her eyes, concentrating on nothing except the blissful chill of the ice—and the tender touch of Wade's hand—against her battered cheek.

"How bad is it, do you think?"

Wade made a snapping noise with his mouth. "Let's just say you won't be posing for any magazine covers anytime soon."

Kerri laughed, a bit of the tension she'd held inside all day easing ever so slightly.

"What did you want to talk about?" Wade asked.

All thoughts of relaxation evaporated and Kerri refocused her brain on their situation. "I'm just trying to make sense of everything. I keep running the pieces of the puzzle through my head, but I'm coming up with nothing more than a real mess."

"You and me both."

"Do you think avoiding murder charges is the only reason Tom's being pursued so aggressively?"

They sat quietly for a few moments before Wade spoke. "I think that's reason enough, but I don't think that's the only reason in this case. No."

Kerri sat up, moving away from Wade's touch. She blinked her eyes open, pinning him with a glare.

"Do you know something I don't?"

Wade searched her face, as if he were trying to decide whether or not to tell her something.

There had been only one occasion for Wade to learn any info without her.

"You never told me about your meeting with Michael Chase." Kerri narrowed her eyes at him. "Is it safe to assume that expression you're wearing has something to do with what you two discussed?"

Wade blew out a breath. The muscles in his jaw visibly tightened. "He thinks there's more to the fire than ecoterrorism."

Kerri frowned. "Such as?"

"A conspiracy of some sort. Between Project Liberation and an unknown party."

"An unknown party?" She sat even straighter now, at full attention. "Who? Why?"

"He didn't say who, but whoever it is apparently wants to hurt the Chase family."

Confusion whirled through her. "What would Pine Ridge have to do with the Chase family?"

Wade hesitated for a split second before he spoke. "Vincent Chase used to think of me as a son. Michael thinks the Pine Ridge attack was designed to push Vincent to action. There've been other attacks, but this one's more personal. They want him to strike back."

"At who?" Kerri asked.

He shrugged. "That's the million-dollar question."

"And you believe the son?"

Wade pressed his lips into a tight, tense line. "I'm not sure, to be honest. He never gave me a straight answer." He hesitated for a moment, staring intently at Kerri. "I'd like to talk to Vincent."

She couldn't believe what she was hearing. "What?"

Wade's dark eyes narrowed, but he said nothing.

Kerri shook her head. "If Project Liberation and this other mystery party are trying to draw Vincent Chase into battle, why on earth would you go to see him? Or would you like to invite additional danger into our lives?"

"He could offer protection, as well as answers."

Kerri gave a disbelieving laugh. "You can't be serious. Why would you do this?"

She stood and paced toward the window, anger simmering deep in the pit of her stomach, ready to boil over. Not anger at Wade, but anger at herself.

Just how far was she going to follow this man? How much deeper into harm's way was she going to drag her son?

What had she been thinking when she believed Wade could protect them—protect Tom? But yet, she wanted to believe Wade capable. She wanted to believe that more than anything.

And that was the thing tearing her apart inside.

She'd spent three years blaming Wade for John's death and for dragging John's memory through the mud, yet here she stood, ready to follow Wade wherever he suggested.

She must be insane.

Surely she wasn't thinking with her head.

Wade stood, stepping behind her. He pressed a hand to her shoulder, sending an unwanted awareness simmering to life within every inch of her body.

"I need to know what's going on, Kerri. It's the only way to keep us safe. If we're not aware of who our enemies are, we can't protect ourselves."

He made sense. She had to admit that. But just because his logic made sense didn't mean his planned course of action wasn't dangerous.

"What if the enemy is Vincent Chase?" She turned to face him.

Wade slid his hand from her shoulder to her waist, his features tensing. "He's not the enemy."

"Well then who is?"

"The obvious answer is a rival crime family. New York comes to mind."

Kerri's pulse began to pound, attraction and anger and fear battling for position in her heart. "I'm listening."

"I think there's another possibility."

Kerri waited wordlessly.

"What if someone within the Chase organization wanted to take over? To weaken Vincent's leadership? Maybe that same someone had a deal with the New York family about how things will run without Vincent."

Wade's eyes glimmered with something Kerri could only finger as excitement. The very thought this puzzle excited him scared her to death.

"I need to find out," he continued.

Kerri took a deep breath and bit her lip, unable to speak, not even sure what it was she wanted to say, what she wanted to believe.

Wade took her hands in his. "Vincent Chase will know the answer. He's a wise man."

A sense of defeat overcame Kerri and she blinked away moisture from her eyes. "Do you see what a tangled web this has become?"

Wade nodded.

"I almost wish we could run away from it all and recreate our lives." She gave his hand a squeeze. "Would that be so bad?"

"You said yourself Tom deserves to live his life—his old life. Let me fix this."

"What if you can't?"

"It's either that, or you and Tom live your lives looking over your shoulders. Is that what you want?"

She swallowed, realizing she wasn't terribly crazy about either option, but she could read Wade's determination in his face. He believed going to Vincent

Chase was the right thing. Nothing she might say would sway him now.

"What if this is a setup?" She hated to ask the question, but she had to. He was too close to the Chases to consider the possibility.

"No." He stepped away from her, leaving a chill where his hands had held hers. He paced a tight pattern on the indoor-outdoor carpet, his muscles tense, taut, like a tiger about to pounce. "My gut says I'm right. Trust me."

Trust me.

The desire and protectiveness burning in Wade's eyes when he turned back to face her filled Kerri with a sense of longing she'd never known.

A longing to believe him—fully believe him. To let go of the past and trust him now, in the present.

But was she ready to take that step, to put her heart— and Tom's life—on the line?

"When would you go?" She did her best to force a positive tone.

"Tomorrow."

Tomorrow.

Kerri moved to the sofa, needing to sit down. Worry gripped her, squeezing at her belly. "What if something happens here?"

She flashed back to the man on the boardwalk. Following her and Tom. Pursuing them. So close he could have struck at any moment.

Where was that man now? Was he still in Wildwood?

Or had he tracked McCann to Delaware, thinking he'd find Tom there?

Wade squatted in front of her and cupped her chin in his hand. "Nothing's going to happen. No one knows where we are. No one."

"Except the rental agent."

A sly grin curled one corner of Wade's mouth. "He took cash. And do you think I gave him our actual names?"

Kerri couldn't help but laugh. "You're getting good at this." Her next thought wiped the smile from her face. "What if something happens to you?"

"With Chase?" Wade shook his head. "You're worrying over nothing."

"No? Who shot the man up at the cabin? No one seems to know. He could be out there following us for all we know."

She watched as her words sank in. Wade's expression turned from confident to wary to determined once again.

"I'm going to get us out of this. You have my word." He stroked his thumb across her cheek. "I need you to believe me."

Confusion whirled inside Kerri.

There had been a time in her life when she'd considered Wade's word gold. He'd been her husband's best friend—like a member of their family. She'd thought him to be loyal. Trustworthy.

Then everything had fallen apart.

She gave her head a slight shake. "Don't ask me to do that. I'm not ready."

Wade's gaze narrowed. "I don't believe you. I don't believe you hate me anymore."

He tipped up her chin, searching her eyes. "It's not hate I see when you look at me now."

Kerri blinked and tried to turn away, but Wade held her chin steady, keeping her focus nowhere but on him.

"John's death was an accident. A horrible, tragic accident. If I could turn back time and save him, I would. But I can't."

He ran his hand up to her cheek, cupping her face. She leaned into him, wanting so badly to lose herself in his touch.

Her gaze never left his face, focusing on every word he said.

"I shouldn't have marred his memory by testifying to his negligence." True remorse shone in Wade's eyes as he spoke. "I should have left it alone. My pride hurt you, hurt your family."

He lifted his other hand, cradling her face between his palms now. "I need you to forgive me, Kerri."

She swallowed, conflicting emotions ripping her apart inside.

Wade raised up on his knees, pressing his lips to hers. She gave over control, welcoming his kiss, her tongue tangling with his.

But he broke away from her, leaving Kerri more than a bit breathless:

"I need to hear you say it." His voice had gone husky, softer.

Could she forgive him?

Her mind raced through all they'd experienced together since the Pine Ridge fire. How he'd focused on nothing but Tom's safety. How happy her son looked whenever he was with Wade.

How alive inside she felt for the first time in a long time.

Forgive him?

She realized she already had.

The corners of Kerri's mouth lifted ever so slightly. "I forgive you," she said on the breath of a whisper.

Wade closed his mouth over hers, this time not breaking away, but deepening the kiss, pressing her against him, holding her tight.

He slipped his hands around her waist and lowered her gently to the sofa cushions.

Kerri's belly tightened as deep desire spiraled through her, heat building low and heavy. She lifted her knees to cradle his waist, urging him to press more tightly against her.

She wanted to feel his sharp angles against her own soft curves. Needed to explore his body again and again, every masculine inch.

Wade nuzzled her neck, his soft kisses igniting her insides. "I'll never hurt you again."

Kerri arched against him, letting his lips trail a burning path down her neck to her collarbone. He traced one hand along the curve of her waist, over her hip, then cupped the place between her legs where she ached so intensely for his touch.

A soft moan escaped from deep inside her and Wade lifted his face, smiling devilishly at her before he lowered his mouth to her breast, nipping her lightly through the soft cotton of her T-shirt and bra.

He tightened his grip on her back, pressing her breast into his mouth, his suckling turning harder, rougher, exciting her as no man had ever excited her before.

When he caught the soft hem of her shorts with the fingertips of his other hand, then lightly scraped his fingers up the inside of her thigh, Kerri thought she might scream.

Wade pushed her panties out of his way, plunging two fingers inside her, boldly, firmly, stroking her as his lips and teeth teased her nipple.

Kerri writhed beneath him, winding her fingers through his hair, pressing his mouth more tightly to her breast. She arched her pelvis against his exploring fingers, urging him more deeply inside her.

"Wade," she murmured. "Hurry."

Hot desire coiled within her, her body begging for release.

"Not yet," he whispered.

He slid his hand from her back to her stomach, lifting his mouth long enough to move her T-shirt and unclasp her bra in one swift motion.

When his lips covered her nipple this time, hot and wet against her exposed skin, Kerri's first orgasm ripped through her, stunning her in its intensity, leaving her dizzy and weak.

Still Wade's fingers stroked against the ultrasensitive folds between her legs, pushing inside her, bringing her to the edge of a second release.

When he rolled away from her to shimmy out of his jeans, he left her body not cool from his missing touch, but scorching hot in anticipation of what was to come.

He sheathed himself as Kerri slid her shorts over and off her legs.

When Wade lowered himself on top of her, she was more than ready for the sensation of his weight and hardness pressing against her.

He entered her gently, then immediately ratcheted up the intensity of his strokes, his palms splayed to either side of Kerri's head.

She matched his moves, thrusting against him. When his eyelids hooded his darkened eyes, she studied him, their gazes locking, holding, as first his body, then hers, pulsed with release.

Wade dropped his head, burying his face against her shoulder as he groaned with pleasure.

Kerri bit back her own moan, not wanting to wake Tom from his sound sleep.

When Wade dropped onto Kerri, wrapping his arms around her, his eyes were already half-shut. The blissful expression of a totally relaxed man spread across his face, and Kerri smiled inwardly.

At least for just this little while, they'd provided each other with nothing but sheer pleasure. Pure physical release.

She waited for Wade's breathing to go deep and steady before she eased from beneath him. She refastened her bra, pulled down her T-shirt and stepped back into her panties and shorts.

She plucked an afghan from the back of a chair and covered Wade with the fuzzy material, tucking the soft edges around him.

She peeked in on Tom, only to find him sound asleep, his nose whistling slightly with each deep breath. She pressed a soft kiss to his forehead then tiptoed out of the room, closing the door behind her.

Then she made her move.

KERRI HEADED for the boardwalk, knowing it might be foolish to venture out so late at night, but after making love to Wade, she felt blissfully at ease.

She knew the sensation wouldn't last, but she intended to savor the feeling for as long as it did.

She'd always loved watching the ocean at night. Loved listening to the crash of the surf against the sandy beach.

Her breath caught as she neared the top of the ramp, a wide expanse of moonlit ocean coming into view.

Spectacular.

The almost-full moon hung low over the pitch-black ocean. Ripples of light shimmered in the moon's reflection, stretching from the horizon to the very edge of the surf.

The smell of brine filled the night air, and the humidity caused Kerri's skin to go damp.

She leaned against the ocean railing, for the moment ignoring the weight of Wade's cell phone in her pocket. At this particular instance in her life, she wanted nothing more than to savor the magnificent view and the satiated feeling making love to Wade had provided.

She stood and stared for several minutes, then shook herself from the trance. She hadn't sneaked out only for the moonlight, after all.

She had a call to make.

The clock radio in the bungalow's kitchen had read ten forty-five just before she'd left. Too late to make a call to a client under normal circumstances, but these were no normal circumstances.

She turned north, walking away from the noise of the amusement pier. The bungalow they'd rented sat on the fringe of Wildwood's expansive collection of amusements and stores. After just a few minutes, she'd put enough distance between herself and the pier to minimize the level of background noise.

Kerri slipped her address book from her back pocket, finding her client's number and repeating it out loud. She pulled Wade's cell from her front pocket and punched in the numbers, hesitating before she hit the send button.

As far as the outside world is concerned, you and Tom are gone.

McCann's warning reverberated through her brain, but she silenced his words, silenced his voice.

She pressed the send button and waited. Her client answered on the fourth ring, sounding a bit hesitant to be taking such a late-night phone call.

"Mrs. Monroe, it's Kerri Nelson. I'm so sorry to call you this late, but there's a problem with the sculpture."

She went on to explain she'd be unable to deliver the piece on time and would return all monies paid. When questioned, she fabricated a story about an ill relative who needed round-the-clock care.

Mrs. Monroe was in the middle of expressing her distinct displeasure when a group of teens skateboarded past Kerri, whooping and hollering as they zoomed by.

"What on earth is that racket?" Mrs. Monroe asked.

"I'm sorry. Just some kids from the pier."

Kerri winced as soon as the words left her mouth.

The pier.

She made yet another apology then quickly disconnected the call.

As she headed back toward the bungalow, she mentally berated herself. How could she be so stupid as to mention the pier? How many piers were there along the coast?

But then she caught herself, forcing logic into her brain.

Mrs. Monroe didn't care about Kerri's location. She only cared that she'd be without a sculpture for her upcoming event.

As she pushed open the bungalow's front door, Kerri shoved the thought out of her head,

Lord knew a slip of the tongue in a call to Mrs. Monroe was the least of her worries.

Once she returned Wade's cell phone to the pocket of his jeans, no one would ever know what she'd been up to.

Chapter Thirteen

Wade left before ten the next morning, promising to be back just as soon as he'd met with Vincent Chase. He made Kerri give her word that she wouldn't leave the bungalow under any circumstance, then he'd driven away without a backward glance.

When the knock sounded at the door an hour later, Kerri knew it couldn't be Wade. He hadn't been gone long enough, unless he'd changed his mind and come back.

Her pulse quickened at the thought. Maybe he'd decided starting over was safer than digging themselves any deeper into the maze of danger they'd stumbled into.

She and Tom shared a puzzled look, but Kerri held a finger to her lips, signaling her son to stay quiet.

The doorknob rattled and her heart caught, her insides going liquid.

What if the killer had found them, found their location? What if he'd never expected them to leave Wildwood at all? He'd been one step ahead of them since the nightmare began, why should she expect anything different now?

The knock sounded again, this time louder, more menacing—an incessant pounding that rattled her teeth and set her nerves on edge.

She gripped Tom's arm and pulled him down the hallway toward the bedroom. They'd escape. They'd climb out a window. They'd hide until Wade came back.

Something.

Anything.

Tom's eyes had gone huge with fright, and she knew her actions were doing nothing to ease her son's fears.

"Kerri," a male voice boomed through the door. "It's Adam McCann. I need to speak with you."

She and Tom stopped in their tracks, and she pulled her son to her, pressing his head against her chest, her mind racing through the possibilities.

Did the voice sound like McCann's?

She'd only spoken to him twice, but she thought she recognized him.

"It's urgent, Kerri. It's about Wade."

Wade.

Her heart fell to her toes, and she pushed Tom into the bedroom.

"Lock this door and do not come out until I tell you to." She gave his shoulders a quick shake. "Understand? You do not open this door for anyone but me. Not anyone. Got it?"

Tom nodded and swallowed, his complexion going pale.

Kerri waited until she heard the lock click, then

headed for the front door. When she flipped the dead bolt and yanked the door open, McCann held his fist in the air, poised to pound again.

He dropped his hand to his side and gave her a grim expression.

"Is Wade hurt?" she asked, her heart tapping rapidly against her ribs.

McCann shook his head. "Not that I know of. But he isn't the man you think he is."

Kerri blinked, disbelief wrapping itself around her brain. What was he talking about? And how had he found them?

"May I come in?" McCann asked.

He'd already crossed the threshold, apparently determined to drop whatever bombshell he felt compelled to share.

Kerri stepped back and wrapped her arms around herself. A chill spread across her shoulders and up the back of her neck.

Her instincts screamed that she didn't want to hear— didn't want to know— whatever it was that Detective McCann was about to tell her.

But based on the set of the man's expression, she had no choice.

Kerri sank into a kitchen chair and braced herself.

WADE DROVE NORTH on the parkway, hooking a U-turn through a rest stop and taking the southbound exit for Sea Isle City, just as Vincent had directed.

Earlier that morning, he'd thought about changing his mind and skipping the meeting with Vincent. Maybe Kerri was right. Maybe he'd be achieving nothing more than increasing their risk. He'd actually thought about what she'd said—about running, changing identities, starting over.

Then he'd reminded himself that Kerri and Tom deserved a normal life. They couldn't run forever.

It was then Wade realized their safety and happiness mattered far more than the sainted reputation—as Michael Chase called it—that he'd cultivated and protected all these years.

If he had to ask Vincent Chase for help, he'd do it. Even if that meant losing Kerri's respect...hell, losing Kerri. She and Tom were all that mattered, whether he ended up in their lives or not.

Wade drove toward the ocean, carefully watching for the unmarked turnoff Vincent had said would come before the marina. He scanned the tall marsh grasses lining the sandy shoulder and then spotted an opening. Just ahead.

He maneuvered carefully, feeling the slip of the car's tires as he pulled onto the sandy road. Even though the man had once been like a father to him, Wade couldn't deny the adrenaline his nerves sent zinging through his system at the thought of seeing Vincent Chase, New Jersey crime boss.

It wasn't every day you were told to look for a black sedan next to the back bay, but there it sat, so out of place among the tourists and fishermen, it wasn't funny. But then, Vincent had never been one to blend in.

Wade pulled alongside the sedan and the driver's window slid down.

"Get in."

The window began its ascent before Wade got a good look at the man behind the wheel. He had one impression, though.

Big.

Wade did as he was told, cutting the ignition then climbing from the driver's seat. He pulled open the back door of the sedan and slid onto the rich leather seat. Vincent Chase sat waiting, smiling, a genuinely happy expression painted across his face.

"Wade, my boy." He held out his arms for an embrace. "It's been too long."

Wade quickly hugged the man, a swirl of memories warming his insides. When he sat back he felt guilty for waiting until he needed something from Vincent before getting in touch. It had been a long time since the two had seen each other, let alone sat down to talk.

Vincent's expression morphed from joyful to intense in the blink of an eye. "I'm sorry for your troubles. I know how hard you worked to get the zoning approvals for Pine Ridge."

Pine Ridge.

Disappointment nipped at the back of Wade's brain. He'd been so caught up in protecting Tom and unraveling the mystery of just who was involved in the arson that the fire's end result paled in importance. His prized project had been completely destroyed, yes, but suddenly there were two far more important concerns in his life.

Kerri and Tom.

He forced a tight smile. "I'll rebuild."

Vincent patted his hand. "I know you will. You never were a quitter. Not in all the time I've known you."

Wade decided not to waste any more time. He needed to question Vincent and get back to the bungalow.

He slid his hand from beneath Vincent's. "I get the distinct impression there's more involved here than ecoterrorism."

The older man merely donned a puzzled expression.

"And I also get the impression you know exactly what I'm talking about," Wade continued.

Vincent nodded slowly then narrowed his pale gray eyes. "Let's just say I've kept abreast of the situation. Yours is not the only site that's been hit."

"I understand there've been more hit up north."

Vincent nodded again, this time with a look of displeasure.

"Yours?" Wade asked.

Another nod, this one tight and quick.

"Why?"

"Territory." He shrugged. "Sometimes the families aren't much more civilized than dogs, I'm afraid."

Myriad thoughts swirled through Wade's mind. Had

he been correct about the New York family's involvement? Was that what Vincent meant?

"The New York family?" Wade asked.

Vincent nodded.

"They're targeting your construction sites?"

This time there was no nod. No expression other than a narrowing of the older man's eyes. "That's all you need to know, and when you step out of this car, I want you to forget I told you."

"Why Pine Ridge? Because of our past?"

"Sorry, son. People know I got you started, and they know how I feel about you."

Wade let out a frustrated sigh. He'd dragged Tom into testimony not just against a Project Liberation arsonist, but one tied to the New York crime family. What a fool.

"They're trying to draw me out." Vincent made a tsking noise with his mouth. "I'll come out when I'm ready to come out." He pointed at Wade. "But you need protection. And the kid needs protection."

"I've got it taken care of."

"By hiding in some ratty old bungalow in Wildwood?"

The leather creaked behind Wade as he sat back, disbelief washing through him. "How—"

"Never think people can't find you, my boy." He paused dramatically. "They can."

Dread tugged at Wade's gut. "How did you...?"

The older man smiled. "I've got my best man on you."

"You're having me followed?"

Vincent nodded.

Wade flashed back on his meeting with Michael and his unwillingness to give Wade the full story.

"Michael?"

Vincent nodded again, amusement glittering in his eyes.

"The shooter up at the cabin?" Wade asked.

"If not for him, your witness would be dead, and Ms. Nelson would be a grieving mother."

Vincent's words settled over Wade, chilling him to the bone. The man was right.

Wade had been so sure he could be the ultimate protector, yet he'd let Kerri and Tom down.

"You saved the mother," Vincent said, as if reading his mind. "They'd both be dead without you and Michael. Sometimes you need backup. Like now."

Wade sat silently, working through everything Vincent had told him, trying to understand the larger picture.

"Why would Project Liberation join with the New York family?"

"Money." Vincent shrugged with his eyes. "It's what makes the world go around, my boy. They perform jobs for the family and the family provides them with the cash they need for their tree-hugging activities."

Wade hesitated before speaking, unsure whether or not he was ready to broach the one subject to which he needed a straight answer. He leaned toward Vincent.

"Are you sure no one on the inside is involved in this? What if this is a setup to take you down?"

The concern in Vincent's eyes turned into anger.

Cold, hard anger. "No one in the Chase organization would turn against me, especially not my son, if that's what you're thinking."

It was, but Wade hadn't wanted to be so bold as to say so.

"But it wouldn't be the first time a son went against a father. Maybe to join forces with the New York group? For power?"

Vincent tapped on the glass dividing the front and back seats then extended his hand to Wade. "It's been wonderful to see you. If you want to take the family's protection to the next level, you know where to find me. In the meantime, Michael will never be too far away."

The passenger door opened, and the driver reached for Wade's arm before he could say so much as a goodbye. The driver slammed the door shut once Wade had stepped clear, then he climbed behind the wheel and took off in a burst of sand.

Wade hurried back to Kerri's car, his conversation with Vincent Chase spinning through his mind.

Project Liberation had torched Pine Ridge under orders of the New York family in an effort to hit Chase at a personal level. So who was after Tom? The family? Project Liberation? Or both?

Vincent obviously felt there was no one inside his organization who'd been disloyal, but what if he were mistaken?

He'd assigned Michael to protection duty, but what if Michael were the rogue inside the family? Who better would know that hitting Wade would affect Vincent personally?

All of Michael's actions might have been taken to lull Kerri and Tom into a false sense of security. What if his moves had been made merely to set up the final takedown?

He'd known their location every step of the way.

Like right now at the bungalow in Wildwood.

Where Kerri and Tom were sitting ducks.

Michael obviously hadn't followed Wade here. He'd stayed behind, knowing Wade would be out of the picture.

"Damn it."

Wade cranked on the ignition and made an abrupt U-turn, fishtailing in the sand as he raced back toward the main road.

Trepidation twisted his gut, but determination filled him.

He needed thirty minutes to get back to Kerri and Tom, but what if they didn't have thirty minutes?

He'd left his cell phone back at the bungalow, in case of emergency. He could search for a pay phone, search for a place from which to call and warn them, but could he afford to lose another minute?

Wade made a gut decision, pulling the car onto the parkway and pressing the accelerator to the floor. He'd risked discovery by taking the parkway north to the meeting, and now he again risked the car being spotted, but he had no choice. He had to get back to Wildwood as quickly as possible.

For all he knew, he might already be too late.

KERRI GESTURED toward the chair next to her. "Would you like to sit, detective?"

McCann shook his head. "No, thanks. It's better if I stand."

A part of Kerri wanted to show her strength by standing toe to toe with the man, but she stayed where she was, wanting the security of the chair beneath her as she waited for him to say whatever it was he was about to say.

McCann stared at her and thinned his lips, as though he were trying to decide how to begin. "Has Wade told you about his affiliation with the Chase family?"

Kerri swallowed and nodded. "He told me he grew up with them. He and Michael were friends and that Vincent was like a father to him."

McCann took a step closer, leaning a bit toward Kerri's chair. "Did he tell you Vincent Chase bankrolled his company?"

Kerri's heart began to pump a bit faster. "Wade's company?"

Surely McCann had to be mistaken. If Wade were financially involved with the Chases, he would have told her. Wouldn't he?

"Sorenson Construction." McCann nodded, then scrubbed a hand across his face. "We've been keeping an eye on him for a long time."

Confusion spun in Kerri's mind. "I thought you two were friends."

McCann cocked one brow toward his hairline. "You

know what they say. Keep your friends close and your enemies closer."

Kerri slumped against the back of her chair, having difficulty wrapping her brain around what the detective was saying.

"We have reason to believe Wade's company is a front for the Chase family," McCann continued.

She tipped her head, wondering if she were hearing correctly. "Organized crime? You want me to believe Wade is involved in organized crime?"

"We think Pine Ridge was hit in an effort to draw the Chase family into battle."

"I thought it was an act of ecoterrorism?"

"So did we. Initially. But now we have reason to believe Project Liberation is working with the New York mob to take down the Chase family."

McCann's expression grew even more serious than it already had been. "There's more."

More? She didn't think she could bear to listen to any more.

She'd trusted Wade with her son's safety—with his life. She'd believed his development had been the target of crazed environmentalists when she agreed to let Tom testify. Wade had acted as though he'd believed the same thing.

Had Wade knowingly encouraged Tom to testify against the mob?

Was he insane?

"Kerri?" McCann touched a hand to her shoulder. "Are you all right? Can I get you some water?"

She took a deep breath and bit down on her lip. "I'm fine." She lifted her gaze to his expectantly.

"Most of the guys on the force think your husband had uncovered something on Wade."

John?

The room spun and Kerri gripped the table.

"Incriminating evidence," he continued. "We've never been able to prove it, but have reason to believe Wade arranged for your husband to have an accident before John could expose the true extent of Wade's link to the Chase family."

Kerri felt as though McCann's words had let the air out of her lungs. She leaned forward, lowering her face to her hands. A shiver ripped through her and her heart ached.

How could she have believed Wade? She'd trusted him, made love to him. She'd finally forgiven him for John's death.

All for what? To be told everything she believed about the man was a lie?

He'd deceived her from day one, and he'd knowingly thrust Tom into a life-threatening situation. For what? To get justice for himself? To keep his name in the clear? *What?*

The man had practically lived at their house before John's death, yet she'd never suspected his involvement in organized crime. Not once.

Now McCann stood before her telling her Wade was

not only part of the Chase family but that John's death hadn't been an accident at all.

She never should have let Wade back into their lives—even worse, into their hearts. Every time Tom looked at the man, his eyes gleamed with hero worship.

As for her, she'd actually thought she might be falling in love with the man.

"I'm sorry, Kerri." McCann's voice took on a gentle tone, something she hadn't thought him capable of. "I need to get you out of here. Right now. You and Tom.

"I'll take you where the Chase family and Wade can't harm you. Tom will be safe until we've made an arrest. You have my word."

She lifted her chin, studying the man intently. One question had been lurking in the back of her mind ever since he'd crossed the threshold.

"How did you find us?"

Surprise flashed across his features, as if she'd shocked him with her blunt question. Just as quickly, his expression grew serious again.

"The call you placed from Wade's cell."

He'd traced her call to Mrs. Monroe? How?

"You can tap a cell phone?"

He nodded. "We tracked incoming and outgoing calls, and Mrs. Monroe was more than happy to tell me you'd called from a pier when I explained it was a matter of life or death."

A matter of life or death.

Kerri felt the blood rush from her face.

"But it could have been any pier, any house."

"I took my chances that you'd come back to Wildwood." McCann furrowed his forehead as if the question was a no-brainer. "Then I questioned Realtors. How many people do you think rent a house for the weekend using cash? Trust me. You weren't difficult to find."

Fear tugged at Kerri's insides. If McCann had tracked her so easily, the killer could have done the same.

McCann was right.

She and Tom had to leave now. Right this moment.

"All right." She nodded, jumping to her feet and heading toward the bedroom door. "We'll do whatever you say, just promise me you'll keep Wade Sorenson away from me and my son. For good."

"You have my word."

Something in McCann's tone sent a chill up Kerri's spine, but she shook it off, attributing it to the shock her system had just taken.

She knocked gently on the bedroom door. "Tom, honey? It's me. Open up."

The moment she looked at her son's pale face she knew he'd overheard every word. Tears swam in his eyes and blotches of pink had fired in his cheeks.

Anger flared inside her.

How dare Wade Sorenson do this to her son. At that moment, looking down into Tom's broken-hearted expression, she wanted to strangle Wade with her bare hands.

She pulled Tom into her arms. "I'm so sorry, honey."

He sniffled. "I trusted him. He said I was doing the right thing."

Kerri pushed him to arm's length and focused solely on his eyes. "You are doing the right thing. I was wrong to tell you not to come forward. Seeking justice is always the right thing if you do it for the right reasons."

Her voice faltered and she paused for a moment, working to control her fury in front of her son. "Daddy would have wanted you to do the right thing. For the right reason. Never forget that."

Tom sniffed again, and Kerri gave him another quick hug. "Come on. Detective McCann's waiting. He's going to take us away from here to somewhere safe."

Her son nodded, not uttering another word as they walked down the hall.

Kerri glanced at Wade's cell phone where it sat on the coffee table and fantasized about slamming it against the wall. She should be thankful, actually.

Using his cell phone had led Detective McCann to their hiding place and very well may have saved their lives.

She held Tom's hand as McCann opened the front door, stepping aside to let them walk ahead. His unmarked cruiser sat in front of the house and if Kerri weren't mistaken, another man sat in the passenger seat.

She squinted, but could only make out a figure, not a face.

Along for backup, she imagined.

Crack.

A shot rang out and Kerri instinctively pushed Tom to the ground. McCann was on her in an instant, gun drawn, pulling her to her feet and shoving her and Tom toward the car.

A dark-haired man appeared in the street, gun trained on McCann.

The killer. It had to be the killer.

If he shot McCann, Tom would be a sitting duck.

"Move," McCann ordered.

Kerri did as she was told.

"It's over, McCann." The dark-haired man's voice boomed with authority.

Kerri reached for the back door handle just as McCann fired off a shot. The dark-haired man went down, hitting the street with a thud.

"Get in." McCann was behind her now, pushing hard.

"Run!" the downed man called out.

What?

Kerri pulled open the door, pushing Tom ahead of her. Her heart hammered in her chest, her pulse roared in her ears.

Tom ducked his head, glanced into the front seat and froze.

"Get in," McCann repeated, his voice missing all trace of the gentleness he'd displayed earlier.

But Tom said nothing. He did nothing.

He stood, bolted to the spot.

"Mom."

His voice was so soft Kerri wondered if she'd imagined it. "What?"

He straightened now, tightening his grip on her hand. He turned to face her, his eyes full of fear.

"It's him."

McCann had pulled open the driver's door, apparently assuming Kerri and Tom were about to climb in the back. But Kerri ducked her head and looked at the man in the front passenger seat. The man the sketch artist had drawn.

The man Tom had seen at Pine Ridge.

The man who had beat her mercilessly.

Her stomach flipped and she gripped Tom's hand—hard—then looked her son right in the eye.

"Run."

Chapter Fourteen

Kerri and Tom took off, racing straight for the board-walk. If they could reach the boardwalk—reach the crowds—they'd have a chance.

A shot rang out. Then a second.

Kerri flinched, waiting for the pain, but nothing happened. She glanced at Tom as they ran. "You're all right?"

"Yeah."

They scrambled up the ramp to their only chance for escape, the throng of tourists covering the boardwalk. As they rounded the top of the railing and dashed toward a line of stores, Kerri risked no backward look, focused only on outsmarting McCann.

McCann.

She couldn't process the reality of it all, yet she shouldn't have been so surprised. His guilt explained everything.

The initial leak about Tom's identity.

The attacks at the cabin.

His determination to track them down today.

The rogue on the inside.

But why?

Had Wade been right? Was the Chase family innocent in the entire affair?

And what about everything McCann had just told her? Truth? Or more lies?

She gripped Tom's hand and pulled him into a T-shirt shop, controlling the only thing she could. Running for their lives.

Overflowing racks pressed one against the other, each sporting neon, hand-lettered signs announcing end-of-summer deals.

Kerri and Tom weaved in and out of the maze of racks, knocking shirt hangers to the floor, careening into shoppers, working to make their way toward the back of the store.

There had to be a backroom.

Had to be an exit.

Kerri was counting on it.

She spotted a door and gave Tom's hand a tug. "Hurry, honey. We'll cut out the back and lose them."

His face had lost all color except for the circles of pink their running had caused. His eyes were the size of saucers and Kerri's heart caught.

Her son was terrified.

Absolutely terrified.

She longed to pull him into her arms, to comfort

him, to reassure him everything would be all right, but there wasn't time.

There wasn't time for anything but running for their lives.

"Hey, you can't go back there," a salesgirl called out as Kerri pushed the office door open and dragged Tom into a room even more crowded than the store itself.

She hadn't thought it possible.

Adrenaline buzzed through her system, yet she felt as though they were moving in slow motion.

"Hurry." She urged Tom along as she frantically searched for a way out.

There *had* to be a way out.

Then she saw it. A larger door and the metal bar that spelled freedom.

She pressed against the bar with all of her might, wincing when an emergency alarm sounded so shrilly above her head she thought her brain might explode.

"Mom!" Tom yelled, stopping in his tracks.

"Keep running!"

Kerri gave his arm a yank and pulled him out onto a set of concrete steps that led down to the asphalt drive behind the boardwalk.

They raced down the steps, side by side, turning underneath the boardwalk, toward the promise of hiding places and survival.

The alarm continued to sound and voices shouted above the din.

Loud voices.

Male voices.

Kerri's heart seized in her chest and she tightened her grip on Tom, racing forward.

So much for her plan to make a quiet getaway.

She might as well have painted a huge sign that said, This way to Kerri and Tom.

Tom stumbled and fell, one knee digging into the damp sand. Kerri's grip was too tight to let go in time and he screamed in pain and grabbed his shoulder.

My God. Had she dislocated his shoulder?

Tom scrambled to his feet. Kerri placed one hand on his shoulder and held his hand with the other.

"Hang on, honey. This might hurt like heck for a minute, but then it'll be all right. I promise."

Kerri rotated his arm, praying she hadn't pulled it out of his socket. Tom winced, but his arm had full mobility.

Tom nodded. "Better."

The voices grew louder, and Kerri could distinctly make out McCann's.

Damn it.

They'd lost time with Tom's injury.

If they ran now, they'd be spotted instantly.

She frantically scanned the area beneath the board-walk for a place to hide, settling on the most obvious thing. The mammoth wooden pilings.

She and Tom raced toward the closest edge of the boardwalk, lunged behind a piling and ducked.

Kerri held her son tight in her arms, feeling his heart pound beneath the palm she splayed against his chest to hold him close. Her own heart beat so loudly she was sure McCann and the killer would hear her.

The two men raced into her line of vision and she pushed Tom lower to the sand, willing him not to move.

Thankfully, the sand underneath the boardwalk was covered in millions of footprints and indentations. McCann would have no luck singling out their prints.

She held her breath as the men raced past, shouting orders back and forth to one another. When they raced up a distant set of stairs and back onto the boardwalk, Kerri released her breath, pressing her mouth to Tom's ear.

"Let's go."

They raced back in the direction from which they'd come, headed for the amusement pier.

She could only hope McCann and the other man wouldn't double back. Once she and Tom committed to the pier, there'd be no turning back, no other direction in which to run.

They'd be sitting ducks.

WADE TURNED THE CORNER, headed for the bungalow, but slammed on his brakes as soon as he'd made the turn. A body lay in the street and McCann's sedan sat apparently deserted, doors flung wide open.

Wade slammed Kerri's car into Park and jumped from his seat, not taking the time to cut the ignition.

His heart jackhammered and his insides rolled.

He was too late.

Damn it, he was too late.

He raced toward the downed man and stopped short as recognition set in.

Michael Chase.

Had he been the protector? Or the aggressor?

Michael had shrugged out of his jacket and was struggling to use the fabric to stem the flow of blood from his wound. Wade took over, applying as much pressure as he could to Michael's shoulder wound.

"Where are Kerri and Tom?" The frantic tone of his voice bordered on desperate, but he didn't care. He *was* desperate.

Michael grimaced in pain, moving to speak. "McCann."

"Did he shoot you? Did he take them to safety?" Wade scanned the area but saw no one else. No movement. Nothing. "Did you come after them, you bastard?"

"Protect them," Michael ground out through clenched teeth as he shook his head.

"Then where are they?" Wade tightened the pressure on Michael's wound and the man cried out.

"After them. Just happened. Hurry."

That explained the lack of onlookers or police, but who was after who? Wade only cared about one thing.

"Where are Kerri and Tom?"

"McCann," Michael repeated, his voice fading. "After them."

Relief surged through Wade. McCann was out to help Kerri and Tom, to save them from whoever had shot Michael.

"Who shot you?"

"McCann."

For a split second everything around Wade—sound and motion—froze, as the name Michael had spoken registered in his brain.

"McCann shot you?" His voice climbed an octave, dripping with shock.

"The leak." Michael's eyes closed momentarily, then blinked open. "On the inside."

Reality crashed down on Wade like a ton of bricks. McCann was the one person who had known every move. From beginning to end. He'd manipulated every step of the game except the relocation to Wildwood.

McCann was the rogue on the inside.

"He's working with Project Liberation?" Wade climbed to his feet. He hadn't a moment to spare.

Chase nodded. "With Flame."

"What?" Wade's mind raced, frantically trying to make sense of what Michael was saying.

"Freelancer. Arson. With McCann." Chase spoke slowly, fighting to enunciate his words.

Fury tangled with the panic spiraling through Wade's gut. "Why didn't you tell me? Damn it. You let me put Tom right in his lap."

"Had. To. Draw. Him. Out."

Wade bit back the urge to punch a man who was already down. His mind raced, adrenaline pumped through his veins. He had to find Kerri and Tom. Find them before McCann did.

There was no one to protect Kerri and Tom now except for Wade. Michael lay bleeding on the sidewalk and McCann was in pursuit—as the aggressor.

"Already called 9-1-1," Michael whispered.

Wade noted the cell phone on the ground beside him.

"Go." Michael's words were barely audible. "Boardwalk."

Sirens sounded in the distance, drawing nearer. Wade was already in motion. "Help's coming."

"Gun."

Wade stared at the shimmering weapon next to Michael's hand. He back stepped and plucked it from the asphalt, then turned, pushing himself to run as fast as he could toward the boardwalk.

He tucked the gun behind his back and under his T-shirt as he ran.

He didn't know how he'd ever find Kerri and Tom in the huge expanse of the Wildwood boardwalk, but if he had to, he'd die trying.

As he crested the top of the steps, an alarm screamed above the voices and noise of the boardwalk crowd.

Wade's heart leaped with hope.

Maybe—just maybe—the ear-splitting alarm had something to do with Kerri and Tom's efforts to escape.

There was only one way to find out.

KERRI AND TOM raced up the same ramp they'd taken from the house to the boardwalk, the street behind them now filled with police and emergency vehicles.

She glanced back in time to see a stretcher being loaded into an ambulance, but didn't hesitate long enough to get a good look. It had to be the third man. The mystery shooter who had come out of nowhere and tried to stop McCann.

Could it be the same person who had saved Tom at the cabin? But who?

She glanced down the boardwalk as she and Tom turned toward the amusement pier. She could spot no one in particular, just a mob of weekend tourists flooding the boards, wandering, laughing, enjoying the summer sun and the surf just off the edge of the boardwalk.

She wanted to stop and scream. Wanted to tell them all that her son was in danger. That two maniacs were after them, one of them a cop.

A cop.

Who would believe her? If she somehow found the boardwalk's security station, would she find safe haven, or would they believe one of their own? A Homeland Security officer named McCann?

After all, he could flash his badge and fabricate any sort of story he wanted to.

Kerri didn't have that option. Her only option was to find somewhere to hide, wait for the danger to pass, then take Tom and run where McCann would never be able to find them.

The crowds grew thicker as they neared the entrance to the amusement pier. Kerri slowed her pace ever so slightly as they passed beneath the brightly decorated archway.

Was she making a fatal mistake?

She barreled forward, urging Tom along with her. His pace had slowed, their exertion obviously catching up to him. Her own lungs burned, protesting the speed with which they'd been running ever since Tom had recognized the killer.

They dodged in and out of lines of tourists waiting to board rides. For a fleeting moment, she considered jumping on the Ferris wheel or roller coaster, anything to make her and Tom invisible, if only for a few minutes.

Now she was thinking irrational thoughts. She had to snap herself out of it, had to focus.

Kerri stopped running, pulling Tom to a stop beside her. She pivoted, turning slowly in a tight circle, scanning the pier, the crowd, the rides.

Panic began to close in on her.

What if McCann and the other man were behind them?

What if she and Tom were being watched right now?

She had to make a decision. Had to make a move.

But where?

In a maze of people and rides and noises and lights, there seemed to be nowhere to go. Nowhere at all.

Then she saw it.

A warehouse. Set just behind the roller coaster.

"Come on." Kerri lunged forward, dragging Tom along with her. "I found it."

All she had to do now was find a way inside.

WADE TOOK OFF in the direction of the alarm, dodging tourists as they weaved and bobbed in and out of stores and eating establishments.

He followed the sound to a T-shirt shop where a group of sales clerks gathered together, talking and gesturing excitedly.

"Did you have some trouble?" Wade did his best to calm his speech as he talked, but based on the clerks' expression he no doubt had a crazed look in his eye.

A twentysomething brunette pointed a finger toward the back of the store. "This lady and a kid came barging through here, knocking things over and making a mess. Just look at this place."

"Where'd they go?" Wade interrupted.

"Out the back." The girl's features scrunched with her apparent impatience. "Why do you think the alarm's going off?"

"Mind if I check it out?" Wade asked, but he was already in motion, headed for the back exit.

If he could somehow retrace Kerri and Tom's steps, he had a chance of finding them before McCann did, or at least in time to save them.

"They shoplifted, you know."

Wade turned back toward her, shouting his question across the store. "From here?"

She shook her head. "Some other store. The security guards chased them out the back."

Security guards.

No doubt McCann and Flame.

"How many security guards?"

"Two." She pointed again. "They had their guns out and everything. Be careful, it must be pretty crowded under there by now."

As for it being crowded under the boardwalk, he could only hope he'd be so lucky.

Chapter Fifteen

Flame and McCann had split up at Flame's suggestion. The move was common sense actually, although McCann had seemed genuinely impressed by the idea.

Flame often wondered what the New York family saw in the detective, although he imagined they'd settle for anyone they could get on the inside. It had been fortuitous when they'd discovered McCann was a so-called friend of Wade Sorenson. An added bonus, as it were.

The association made the manipulation all the more interesting.

He and McCann had made an agreement to check in by cell phone every five minutes.

McCann headed south, convinced the pair had gone back up on the boardwalk, and continued down the strip of stores and restaurants.

Flame knew better.

He headed toward the closest amusement pier.

After all, hadn't that been where he'd so easily found— and followed—the mother and son the day before?

The closest pier was back in the direction from which they'd first run. Some logic might dictate backtracking was for fools, but Flame had another opinion on the subject.

The mother and son had returned to Wildwood, thinking they could fool him and McCann by *not* running. They'd returned to almost the exact spot where they'd stayed previously—give or take a few blocks.

He had no doubt they'd utilize an identical rationale today, backtracking past the house to the amusement pier.

Flame headed in that direction now, strolling leisurely, quite confident in his decision.

He pictured McCann racing down the boardwalk, frantically searching storefronts. Similarly, he pictured the mother and son, running for their lives, panic painted across their lovely features.

The archway entrance to the pier came into sight and he smiled. He was closing in now.

The street where the shooting had taken place sat littered with emergency vehicles. If these local cops were anything like other shore towns, nine out of ten officers had probably been hired only for the summer months. They wouldn't know the first thing about closing down the area to search for the shooter.

Even if they did, how likely was it that they'd trust the word of Michael Chase? The man was a known criminal. No matter what Chase said, Flame would bet every single responding officer would peg the shooting as a mob hit—and be overjoyed to have the man in custody.

McCann's abandoned vehicle might be a little more difficult to explain. By the time the local police got anywhere with that part of the investigation, Flame planned to be well on his way out of town, his job complete.

He could almost smell the kill, imagining the boy's face before he pulled the trigger.

He drew in a deep, cleansing breath of salt air and glanced momentarily at a group of seagulls as they circled a small child holding a piece of bread.

This entire affair had brought out a facet of his personality Flame never would have imagined he possessed.

He liked the hunt.

Check that. He loved the hunt.

And he had every expectation he was going to enjoy the kill even more.

KERRI CIRCLED the warehouse completely before she realized there was no easy way in. The two entrance doors were padlocked shut and the only large windows faced the rides.

No possible entrance existed that wouldn't expose them to the most crowded section of the pier.

She gripped Tom's hand and made another circle around the back of the building. Staying behind the structure was better than nothing, but she wanted to find a way inside.

She had to find a way inside.

"There, Mom." Tom pointed excitedly, but Kerri

couldn't see any reason for his enthusiasm. The back wall of the warehouse consisted of nothing but concrete block. Faded and chipped yellow concrete block.

Tom pulled his hand free from hers and ran.

Kerri's chest tightened with fear. "Tom!"

But he kept running, all the way to the far end of the building. Kerri gave chase, frowning when Tom dropped to his knees and began pulling against something at the bottom of the wall.

"What on earth are you—" Her question froze on her lips when she realized what he was up to. "Brilliant," she muttered.

Tom didn't look up, working as frantically as he could to loosen the flood vent from the wall.

"Let me help."

Kerri dropped beside her son, working one edge of the vent cover as Tom attacked the other. The metal screen gave way with a snap, sending them both careening onto their backsides.

"Hot dog." Tom scrambled back to his knees, a grin spread wide across his face. "Come on, Mom."

Kerri eyed the small space, more than a little bit skeptical about her ability to shimmy through. Her son, however, should have no problem.

Perhaps it was better that way. She could get Tom inside, replace the vent screen and no one would be the wiser. She could then run back to the boardwalk to distract McCann and the other man.

Her gut twisted at the very thought of leaving Tom alone.

She couldn't do it. If anything were to happen to him, she'd never forgive herself. Her place was here, with Tom. She'd find some way to fit through the vent if it killed her.

Kerri tipped her chin toward the opening. "Hurry, honey. Let's get inside."

Tom slipped through without an ounce of trouble, his slim hips not even coming close to the sides.

Kerri squatted down, then dropped to her stomach, gripping both sides of the opening.

"Mom."

The urgent tone in Tom's voice sent her mind racing. "Are you all right?"

"Don't forget to grab the screen," he answered. "We have to put it back or else the bad guys will know where we are."

Kerri blinked, then backed away from the opening. She had to remember to buy the kid as many detective novels as he wanted once they survived this. "Smart thinking."

"Thanks."

She smiled to herself. Only Tom would hold on to his manners at a time like this.

She slid the vent cover within easy reach of the opening, then dropped to her stomach again, this time slipping her arms through the opening and working to pull herself through.

The pockets of her shorts caught against the edges

of the concrete and she swore under her breath. There was no way she'd make it through.

But when she looked up into the expectant eyes of her son, she knew she had to try.

"Grab my hands, honey, and pull with all your might."

Tom jumped in front of her, tugging against her arms with such force she thought he might be the one to pull her arms out of their sockets.

On his third try, one pocket of her shorts ripped, but she slid through the space, landing safely inside on the concrete warehouse floor.

Tom let out a whoop, but slapped a hand over his mouth when she shot him a warning glance. She quickly pulled the vent back into place as best she could, then grabbed Tom's hand.

When they turned around to assess the interior, they both stood still for a moment, waiting to adjust to the dim lighting.

"Whoa," Tom said softly.

"Whoa is right."

Kerri couldn't believe her eyes. They'd hit the mother lode of hiding places.

Huge sections of rides littered the space like specters of amusements long forgotten.

Teacups. Tilt-a-whirls. Ferris wheel cars. Sections of roller-coaster track. A row of skee-ball machines lined one wall like soldiers ready to march in formation.

"Creepy," Kerri murmured.

"Cool," Tom answered.

She put a hand to his shoulder and pushed. "Let's go."

They moved toward a far corner of the warehouse, picking their way through discarded bumper cars and mammoth teacups, Ferris-wheel baskets and sections of roller-coaster tracks.

A shiver danced along Kerri's spine, yet she couldn't help but notice the gleam in her son's eyes. He was actually enjoying the moment, apparently having forgotten just how serious the danger was.

She thought about reminding him, then decided she'd take his current bright expression over his terrified expression any day.

"We should hide behind the skee-ball machines, Mom."

Kerri drew a breath in and bit down on her lip. "I was thinking more about climbing into one of those cars."

She pointed to a line of brightly colored tram cars, each offering deep hiding spaces and protective sides.

"No good," Tom answered. "That's the first place they'll look. We need to pick something they wouldn't suspect."

Kerri arched a brow. The kid did have a point.

"What about behind the tilt-a-whirl?" she asked.

"Nope." Tom shook his head.

The small hairs at Kerri's nape lifted. If she didn't know better, she could swear they were being watched, but that wasn't possible. Was it?

She shuddered, an inexplicable chill seeping into her

bones. She gripped Tom's elbow and pushed him forward. "Skee-ball machines it is, honey. You're the expert."

One of the machines had been positioned on its side, probably in order to repair it. Kerri waited while Tom climbed behind it, then she followed, doing her best not to make a noise.

Intellectually, she knew they were still alone in the dark, creepy space, but instinctively she sensed something had gone very wrong.

Had they walked into a trap? Had they been followed? Would they ever get out of this dank, dark warehouse alive?

Kerri got down on her knees behind Tom, doing her best to ignore the scrape of rough concrete against her bare skin. She positioned Tom protectively between her and the machine then wrapped her arms around him. She dropped a kiss to his messy hair and held on tight.

"What do we do now, Mom?" he whispered.

"We wait."

And for the first time since they'd raced away from McCann's car, Kerri let her mind wander back to the topic of Wade Sorenson.

She'd been quick to believe everything McCann said, and now she realized every word had more than likely been a lie designed to lure her into the detective's trap.

Guilt filtered through her. Did she think so little of Wade that she'd believe him capable of being part of the Chase crime family? Capable of having John killed?

She shuddered and pulled Tom even more tightly

against her. McCann had to be lying. He had to be. She suddenly couldn't bear to think anything he'd said had been fact.

She reached for her torn pocket reflexively, but found it empty.

Her heart.

Her breath caught and she panicked, thinking she'd dropped it by the vent. Then she remembered exactly what she'd done.

She'd left the stone back at the house, a physical symbol of leaving Wade behind for good. Now she'd give just about anything to feel the reassuring heaviness of the amethyst in her pocket.

She and Tom needed the good-luck charm now more than ever.

Maybe Wade would have returned by now and found the heart. Found the man shot in the street.

Would he even know where to look to find them?

She squeezed her eyes shut and prayed. She wanted to make things right with Wade. To make life normal again for her son.

If only she'd get the chance.

WADE REACHED the bottom of the steps and hesitated, not sure in which direction to run.

The pattern of footsteps beneath the boardwalk offered no help at all. They contained no pattern. Try as he might, he couldn't pick out Kerri and Tom's prints from the thousands of prints and ridges covering the sand.

Two tracks. That's all he'd hoped to find.

No. Wade gave himself a mental shake.

Make that four.

The slick metal of Michael's gun pressed against his back and adrenaline spiked to life inside him. If he could track down McCann and his associate, he'd make sure they never had a chance to find Kerri and Tom.

He walked aimlessly for several seconds, studying the sand, finally realizing the activity was futile. He'd never get anywhere down here below the boards.

His only option was to climb the stairs back to the boardwalk and search. He dashed across the sand to the closest set of steps, taking them two at a time.

When he crested the top, he slowed, blending into the crowd. He started to walk south, but then stepped clear of the pack, pressing his back to an ice-cream store's front window.

His gut instinct suddenly protested his actions. Could he be going in the wrong direction?

He glanced back in the direction of the house, his gaze landing on the archway to the amusement pier. What was it Tom had said his detective novels would say? That he should do the unexpected? He should double back.

The distant sound of music, rides and laughter filtered to Wade, coming from the pier.

Hadn't Tom wanted nothing else ever since they'd arrived in Wildwood? And wouldn't McCann and Flame more than likely have headed south, just as he had been about to do?

Without giving it another thought, Wade took off, racing north on the boardwalk, keeping his eyes focused on his target.

The amusement pier.

And rescuing Kerri and Tom.

FLAME KEPT BACK, watching from the shadow of the roller coaster as Kerri Nelson forced her way through the small opening at the base of the warehouse wall.

He laughed, not trying in the least to hide his amusement.

He had to give these people bonus points for effort. If he'd arrived a moment later, he might never have found them. Fortunately for him, the mother had reached back for an object just as he'd leaned around the corner of the building.

His sensational hunting skills had scored again.

Flame waited until the mother reached to pull some sort of cover back into place, then he casually strolled around to the front of the building, checking each entrance door.

Padlocked.

Every single one.

He gave a quick shrug then dug in his pocket for his pick. He had the first lock open in a matter of seconds. After all, gaining entrance was just another of the skills he'd perfected in the fire-starting business.

Flame hesitated before he entered, pulling his cell phone from his pocket. He punched the speed-dial button for McCann's cell. The man answered on the first ring.

"They're at the amusement pier, past the house. Inside the storage warehouse. I'll leave a door open for you."

He disconnected without waiting for McCann to utter a single word.

When he stepped inside, it took a few moments for Flame's eyes to adjust to the darkness, but when they did, he frowned. The place was piled floor-to-ceiling with all sorts of amusement pier paraphernalia.

What a stinking mess.

No matter. He had all the time in the world.

It was the mother and son whose clock had just run out.

Chapter Sixteen

McCann stuck out like a sore thumb among the amusement pier crowd. Even from the back, Wade would recognize his friend's expensive suit anywhere.

He laughed bitterly. He'd always wondered where McCann got the money to dress as he did. Well, now he knew. Wade imagined being a source inside the police department—hell, inside the office of Homeland Security—paid handsomely.

Wade was looking forward to knocking McCann off his illegal pedestal for good.

He closed the space between them, yet stayed far enough back from McCann that he could duck out of sight at the slightest sign of movement from the detective.

They wound through the crowd. Around the horde of parents and toddlers swarming the teacups. Past the queue of teens waiting for a turn on the giant roller coaster.

When McCann beelined from the coaster to a long warehouse just behind the mammoth structure, Wade frowned.

What was the detective doing?

Then the pieces clicked into place.

Wade had seen no other spot on the pier for Kerri and Tom to seek cover. The warehouse offered the first hint of any sort of hiding place.

What if McCann had somehow already located them?

What if he were moving in now—for the kill?

When the padlock on one of the entrance doors fell open in McCann's hands, Wade made his move, launching into action. Not caring if anyone on the pier saw what he was doing.

In fact, maybe someone would call the cops.

Lord knew the officers responding to Michael's shooting were taking their time. He hadn't seen a police officer during his entire boardwalk trek.

If he had, he would have grabbed the guy and dragged him along for the chase.

Wade's heartbeat quickened as he ran toward the door, hyperalertness flooding through him, snapping every nerve ending to life.

The door closed, but Wade knew he'd have no trouble gaining entrance. After all, he could see the sunlight reflecting off the lock McCann had so carelessly discarded on the ground.

As Wade saw it, McCann could only be at the warehouse for one of two reasons.

He'd set a trap to lure Kerri and Tom to the location, or he had information that told him they were already inside. Wade wasn't stupid. If Kerri and Tom were inside and McCann knew it, that meant Flame was already here—with Kerri and Tom.

The thought sent fear tripping through Wade's system. He concentrated on using the powerful emotion to rush forward, into the unknown situation and probable battle.

When he reached the heavy metal door, he kicked aside the padlock and eased the door open. When he stepped inside, he was completely unprepared for the change in light, blinded by the transition from bright sunshine to darkness.

"Tough to get your eyes used to it, isn't it, old buddy?" McCann's voice sounded near.

Too near.

Damn it. How could Wade have been so stupid? He'd rushed into the warehouse without giving a single thought to strategy.

"Hands in the air," McCann ordered. "Or did you want me to shoot you first and ask questions later?"

Wade hesitated as the images before him slowly came into focus.

He could make out McCann's figure, gun drawn, stance aggressive. Wade's mind raced. Was there any way to reach for Michael's gun without McCann realizing what he was doing?

"Now, Sorenson," McCann continued. "Or I shoot."

"Where are they?" Wade yelled.

McCann laughed, the cold sound raking over Wade's nerves like fingernails on a blackboard. "You're not going to live long enough to worry about that."

Fury ripped through Wade, and all rational thought escaped him. He lunged forward, hitting McCann at the waist, launching him backward, down onto the unforgiving cement floor.

McCann's gun fired, missing them both. Pieces of insulation showered down onto them from the warehouse ceiling.

Wade rolled off of McCann, pulling Michael's gun from his waistband as he did so, but McCann didn't move. He lay on the concrete floor, bleeding from the back of his head.

Wade scrambled toward him, kicking the gun far out of reach from his hand. When the weapon slid beneath a large section of roller coaster, Wade let loose with a string of expletives. He hadn't planned to leave the weapon anywhere near McCann, but he didn't have the time to go after the gun now.

He had to find Kerri and Tom.

Wade felt for McCann's pulse. It beat strong and steady, but there was no doubt about McCann's state of consciousness. The man was out cold.

"Sweet dreams, old buddy."

For a split second, Wade thought about shooting the man just for good measure, but he couldn't do it. He might be desperate, but he refused to stoop to the heartless level to which McCann had gone.

A loud crash sounded from the far side of the warehouse.

Wade launched himself into a full-out sprint before

he could give another thought to McCann, shifting his focus to one thing only.

Finding Kerri and Tom before it was too late.

FLAME HEARD THE COMMOTION near the entrance. He'd been expecting McCann, but not Sorenson.

He had to hand it to the man. Flame found himself impressed Sorenson had actually tracked them to the warehouse.

Flame kept his own focus trained on the mother and her son. He'd seen them climb behind the arcade machines and had been waiting for them to make another move ever since.

He found the pair brilliantly stupid. Their hiding spot was more original than say, ducking down in a teacup or bumper car, but come on. How well hidden could anyone expect to stay behind a row of machines?

He stepped closer now, sensing the woman was about to react to the commotion on the other side of the warehouse. After all, she couldn't be expected to sit back and do nothing now that she'd heard Sorenson's voice.

That was the thing about human emotions. They created vulnerability.

Flame smiled to himself.

Thankfully, he didn't have that weakness to worry about. He hadn't experienced an emotion in a long time.

No, no. He silently corrected himself. If he weren't mistaken, an emotion fluttered through him at this very moment.

Excitement.

Arousal.

He was on the verge of the moment he'd antici-
pated for days.

The elimination of the witness.

Flame stepped to a more suitable location, watching
for the mother to appear.

He didn't know how long it would take her resolve
to break, but he knew her weakness would ultimately
win out.

When he heard the shot—then the silence—he
smiled again, knowing the woman would expose herself
to check on Sorenson.

She had to.

After all, she was only human.

He raised his pistol and waited, humming softly to
himself.

WHEN KERRI HEARD Wade's voice, she gasped, the
sound reverberating off of the equipment and machines
surrounding her.

"It's Wade, Mom." Tom whispered against her chest.
"He came to save us."

"I know," she answered, longing to spring to her feet
and tell Wade they were there, but knowing she couldn't.

Wade's voice wasn't the only voice she could make
out. The second belonged to McCann.

Her belly twisted and tumbled, her insides going liquid.

They'd been found out. But how?

The second man.

Where was McCann's accomplice? He could be anywhere.

She shivered suddenly.

He could be here. Lurking in the shadows. She hadn't heard a sound before the exchange of voices, but that didn't mean a thing.

Her gut told her she might very well have made a grave error in bringing Tom to the warehouse. Maybe the move had been too obvious.

She mentally chastised herself.

Of course it had been obvious. If anyone had tracked them to the pier, they'd realize there was no other available hiding place.

Kerri had to get Tom out of the warehouse and back out into the open. She had to find the police, no matter what McCann might have told them.

No one would hurt her son with an audience. She'd been a fool to isolate him.

An utter and complete fool.

Crack.

The now familiar sound of a gunshot sent her to the floor, pressing Tom beneath her. She covered her son's body with her own, waiting for another shot, another sound.

None came.

Wade.

Had McCann shot him?

Her throat squeezed with fear and longing. She

couldn't lose him now. Not like this. Not after all they'd been through and all she had yet to say to him.

"Stay here," she whispered in Tom's ear. "I have to help Wade."

Kerri struggled to make no noise as she climbed to her feet, squeezing between two skee-ball machines and out into the open. She headed toward the direction of the gunshot, not knowing who or what she was about to find.

She only knew that if Wade had been hurt, she had to help him. Had to save him.

When a large man stepped into her path, gun trained on her face, it took her brain a split second to realize what had happened and who he was.

She bit back her scream and stopped abruptly, her mind frantically working to sort out her options, but failing to come up with anything.

The man smiled.

The cold, emotionless smile of the man who had attacked her in the woods.

Who had set the fires at Pine Ridge.

Who had come to kill her son.

"Run, Thomas!" Kerri screamed at the top of her lungs. "Run!"

But she heard nothing behind her. No scrambling. No motion.

Was her warning too late? Had McCann gotten to Tom? Had he been knocked unconscious, or worse?

Kerri's heart stuttered to a stop in her chest.

No. They couldn't have come this far to have it all go wrong now. Tom had to be safe. He had to be.

She'd find a way out of here for them both.

They *would* survive.

She couldn't stand here and do nothing.

She refused.

Kerri dove to her side, knocking over a barrel full of skee balls, sending them flying.

The noise reverberated through the huge warehouse and she knew that if Wade were still alive, he'd be on his way toward her at this very moment.

She scrambled to her feet, but lost her footing, stepping on a ball and rolling her ankle.

Kerri screamed out in pain as she went down, clutching her ankle in one hand as she tried to drag herself behind something, anything to provide protection from the killer's gun.

But the man didn't fire. He didn't attack her.

He kept smiling. If she weren't mistaken he'd begun to hum.

Dread settled over her like a damp blanket, seeping into her every muscle and bone.

The killer's eyes danced with amusement.

She swallowed, trying to free the knot of fear that squeezed at her throat.

The man wasn't just evil. He was insane.

And as she stared down the barrel of the madman's gun, Kerri wondered if she'd ever see her beautiful boy alive again.

WADE RACED in the direction of the crash, weaving in and out of parts and machinery and discarded amusement pier rides. When he came up against a solid wall of tram cars, he decided to go up and over. He had no time to go around.

He scrambled over the first car, getting a solid footing, then launching himself up onto a second and a third. Finally, he neared the top of the pile and that's when he saw them.

Kerri. On the ground in obvious pain, holding her ankle, her face twisted with fear and panic.

A man towered above her, gun trained on her face.

Wade suddenly had his answer as to why McCann had entered the warehouse. His accomplice had located Kerri and Tom first.

The man Michael Chase called Flame was a spot-on match to the police artist's sketch of the arsonist, and now he stood poised to pull the trigger.

No. Wade wasn't about to lose Kerri like this.

He crested the top of the pile and pointed Michael's gun at the back of the man's head.

"Drop your gun, or I'll shoot."

But the man merely laughed. A cold, heartless laugh that bounced off the tram cars and skee-ball machines beyond where Kerri lay injured.

"Do it," Wade ordered. "Now."

"Or what?" The man turned in Wade's direction, still holding the gun on Kerri. "Are you going to shoot me?

Don't you think I could pull the trigger before your bullet would ever strike me down?

"Then what?" the man continued. "Are you going to sit up there while you watch her die, or are you going to scramble down and cradle her in your arms as she takes her last breath?"

A motion beyond the skee-ball machines caught Wade's eye, but he kept his focus on Flame, not wanting the man to know someone else was in the warehouse.

Tom?

"I'm only going to say this one more time," Wade barked out, wanting to stall for as much time as possible. "Put down the gun and step away from the woman."

Kerri's assailant shrugged, then grinned. "What fun would there be in that?"

A small figure stood off to the side of Flame, out of his line of vision. Tom. Wade had been correct.

His chest swelled with pride at the boy's bravery, but his stomach twisted with trepidation. What could Tom possibly do to save his mother other than draw Flame's attention?

Tom stooped down, picked up a skee ball and swung his arm back in one smooth motion. He let the ball fly, hitting his mother's assailant square in the shoulder.

The big man staggered and Kerri scrambled for cover. Wade jumped, losing his gun as he fell. He landed full on Flame's back just as the man swung his gun toward Tom.

They careened to the floor, rolling, wrestling, hands fumbling for the weapon.

Pain exploded through Wade's shoulder as Flame slammed him against the concrete, but he pushed back, feeling the unmistakable press of the big man's gun between their chests. He fought for control, battling to pull the gun from the man's hand.

Flame slammed him to the concrete once more and Wade lost his grip, stunned momentarily by the blow.

Flame scrambled free, pivoting toward where Kerri and Tom huddled together. Adrenaline surged through Wade's every muscle and he lunged, hitting the man from the side and taking him down. Hard.

They crashed into the metal frame of a section of roller-coaster track just as Flame's gun fired.

KERRI FROZE, sheer terror washing through her when neither man moved.

Tom sobbed and she held him tight, thanking God for sparing his life. "Are you all right?"

He nodded against her. "Is Wade dead?" he asked softly.

Was he?

Shock numbed her and she pushed Tom back into their hiding place. "Don't come out until I come back for you. Understand?"

Her son nodded, his pale eyes moist with tears and wide with terror.

Kerri scrambled to where Wade and the large man lay motionless. The gun sat just beyond the fingertips of her assailant's hand. Kerri kicked it away, then reached for Wade.

He lifted his head just as she reached him.

"Are you all right?" he asked. "Tom?"

Kerri could barely see through the tears that blurred her vision. She nodded, too overcome by joy and relief to speak.

She helped Wade to his feet, ignoring the pain in her ankle. Wade checked the killer for a pulse, but shook his head. When he pulled her into his arms, she gladly sagged against him, welcoming his strong embrace.

But just as Kerri felt herself relax in the safety of Wade's arms, McCann's voice sent ice flooding through her veins.

"Rule number one. Never leave the bad guy's gun where he can reach it."

Chapter Seventeen

Wade stepped between McCann and Kerri, shielding her from the gun McCann held in his hands. The gun he'd left after McCann had gone down.

Idiot.

Disbelief surged through Wade. This couldn't be happening. Not when they'd come this far.

"It's over, McCann. Flame's dead. Shots have been fired. The police are on their way." Perhaps McCann would see his logic and give himself up.

"The local police?" McCann pursed his lips. "Highly doubtful. My money's on them being so overwhelmed by the crime scene at your bungalow they don't know which end's up." He waved the gun for an instant. "Besides, I'm a cop. Who do you think they're going to believe?"

"A crooked cop." Wade knew he had to keep McCann talking. Had to buy more time while he tried to figure a way out of this. "Why did you do it? Once upon a time you were actually one of the good guys."

McCann shook his head. "I was never one of the good guys, but I happen to be very good at what I do."

McCann's arrogance rang blatant in his tone and Wade seized on the opportunity. The detective would probably like nothing more than to brag about just how good he was.

"Who do you work for?" Wade asked.

McCann reached up to rub his head, but kept the gun trained on Wade's face. "The New York family, but I'm sure you already figured that out. You have been annoyingly persistent in this whole thing."

"And Flame set the fire?" Wade continued.

McCann shot a look to where Flame's body lay. "Pity. The guy was a genius. He could set fire to a place and leave not a single clue behind." He blew out a sigh. "He'll be missed."

"What about Tom?"

McCann shrugged. "Collateral damage."

Fury blinded Wade, but he kept talking, kept asking questions, feeding into McCann's arrogance.

"Why Pine Ridge?" The question Wade suspected he knew the answer to, but needed to hear.

"We weren't getting the response we wanted out of Vincent Chase." McCann shrugged, letting the gun go limp in his hand. "We figured hitting you might motivate the old guy to retaliate. Everyone knows he's got a soft spot for you."

"But it didn't work, did it?" Wade's focus shifted from McCann's answers to the gun in his hand. The gun McCann no longer aimed at any of them.

The man had become so consumed in his bragging that he'd apparently forgotten about shooting them.

When McCann threw back his head and laughed in response to something he'd said, Wade lunged forward. He gripped the hand in which McCann held the gun, slamming McCann backward into the pile of tram cars.

The gun flew to the concrete, where Kerri snapped it up and smiled triumphantly.

Wade wrestled McCann to the floor and pinned his arms behind his back.

"Rule number two. Never underestimate the good guys," he snarled in McCann's ear.

THE POLICE ARRIVED moments after Wade had subdued McCann. Apparently an amusement pier employee had entered the warehouse, heard the commotion and gone for help.

McCann had been correct about the confusion back at the house. The responding officers had fallen all over themselves at the prospect of having Michael Chase at their fingertips.

Kerri and Wade sat together as a paramedic dabbed at a gash on Wade's face. Kerri's ankle had been taped and she now sat with it propped up, yet she never took her eyes from Tom as he answered questions for one of the detectives on the scene.

If Wade weren't mistaken, he'd never seen Tom sit so proudly or so tall.

The kid had performed more bravely than any

detective novel character and Wade felt such pride he thought his chest might burst open.

When the paramedic moved away, Wade reached out for Kerri's hand. "You sure you're okay?"

"No." She let a soft laugh slip over her lips, looking up at him with wide eyes. "But I will be." She tipped her chin toward Tom. "I'm worried about him."

Wade smiled, shaking his head. "Something tells me that kid of yours is going to be just fine."

Kerri nodded. "You're probably right."

Wade reached into his pocket, wrapping his fingers around the item one of the police officers had brought him from the crime scene at the bungalow.

Kerri's amethyst heart.

He set it on her lap, delighted to see the bright smile that lit her face in response.

"You left this back at the house."

Kerri cradled the heart in her palm, gingerly touching the facets with her fingertips. "I was afraid I'd lost this for good."

"Did you think you could get rid of me that easily?" Wade asked.

Kerri shook her head. "No. I know it would take a lot more than ditching my amethyst to leave you behind."

"So what's the verdict?" He frowned, quite sure he wasn't succeeding at all in hiding his worry. "Do you think you might want this back?"

Kerri shook her head, placing the stone in his palm.

When he scowled, she laughed again, then reached for his cheek.

"Why don't you hold on to that?" Her voice turned soft, serious. "That way, as long as I've got you, I'll know my heart's in perfectly good hands."

Epilogue

"Make sure your helmet's on," Wade called out as Tom made his maiden run on his new skateboarding ramp.

Kerri stood by Wade's side, wincing as she watched. "Are you sure this is safe?"

Wade shot her a reassuring glance. Even tense, her beauty took his breath away. Her hair had begun to grow back and she'd had the dark dye stripped out. The red strands were long enough now for her to tuck them behind her ears, which she did whenever she got nervous.

Like now.

"Relax, Red. It's better than riding on curbs."

Kerri cast him a sideways glance. "I'm not so sure."

Wade shook his head at her then gave Tom the thumbs-up. "He's a boy. Let him be a boy."

Kerri let out a chuckle. "I always thought you'd be a good influence, but now I'm not so sure."

Wade anchored an arm around her shoulders and squeezed. "Let me see that ring on your finger."

A wide smile spread across her face as she held her

left hand up to the sunshine, the diamond casting off brilliant sparkles.

"That means you're stuck with me," Wade teased. "So you'd better get used to Tom and me forming a united male front."

"Grr-eat." She drew the word out into two syllables.

They stood companionably as Tom took off, careening down the ramp so quickly his image blurred. Kerri sucked a sharp breath through her teeth, but Wade let out a whoop.

Tom scaled the far side of the ramp, then turned expertly, heading back to the bottom, then back up to the landing ridge.

"Awesome, Uncle Wade." He waved excitedly to where they stood. "Thanks."

Wade returned the wave, then took Kerri by the hand and turned her toward their home, one of the most spectacular in the redeveloped Pine Ridge. His insurance had covered the losses, and he'd decided to regroup—and rebuild.

"That wasn't so painful to watch, was it?" he asked.

Kerri shuddered and made a face. "I'm still holding my breath."

As they headed toward their house and their future together, Wade replayed the months since that day on the amusement pier in his mind.

Michael Chase had made a full recovery, and Kerri had promised to think about inviting Michael and Vincent to the wedding.

Wade had come clean about Vincent Chase's investment in his business, explaining that Chase's start-up loan had been repaid years earlier. All costs since that time had been covered by Wade and Sorenson Construction alone.

Kerri had taken the news like a champ, telling Wade she finally understood why his reputation was so darned important to him.

McCann had entered into a plea bargain agreement that had resulted in several high-level indictments for both Project Liberation and the New York family.

Vincent Chase had reassured Wade that the New York family wouldn't bother him again. The families had reached an agreement about which Wade asked no questions.

McCann had also confessed that John Nelson had worked alongside him on the New York family's payroll. The accident that had taken his life had actually been planned sabotage that backfired.

The revelation had devastated Kerri, but the months since had eased the pain. She'd decided not to tell Tom, wanting his memory of his father to remain pure.

Tom had received a good citizen's commendation from the township and from the governor himself. Tom had worn both medals for weeks until Kerri suggested he might want to hang them on his wall before he wore the ribbons straight through.

All in all, life had returned to normal.

Or rather, a new normal.

"Ready?" Wade asked, holding up an arm to block Kerri from entering the house.

"What are you doing?" Her eyebrows snapped together suspiciously.

"This."

Wade hoisted her into his arms, pressing his lips to hers for a long, leisurely kiss. Then he turned, carrying her over the threshold into their new home—the home in which he planned to give Kerri and Tom the life they deserved.

She tightened her arms around him, then nestled her head between his neck and shoulder. "Oh, Wade. It's beautiful."

"Just like you, Red." He pressed a kiss to her hair. "Welcome home."

* * * * *

Experience entertaining women's fiction
for every woman who has wondered
"what's next?" in their lives.
Turn the page for a sneak preview of a new book
from Harlequin NEXT,
WHY IS MURDER ON THE MENU, ANYWAY?
by Stevi Mittman

On sale December 26, wherever books are sold.

treasures being ten minutes away

Design Tip of the Day

> Ambience is everything. Imagine eating a foie
> gras at a luncheonette counter or a side of
> coleslaw at Le Cirque. It's not a matter of food but
> one of atmosphere. Remember that when
> planning your dining room design.
> —Tips from *Teddi.com*

"Now that's the kind of man you should be looking for,"
my mother, the self-appointed keeper of my shelf-life
stamp, says. She points with her fork at a man in the
corner of the Steak-Out Restaurant, a dive I've just been
hired to redecorate. Making this restaurant look four-
star will be hard, but not half as hard as getting through
lunch without strangling the woman across the table
from me. "*He* would make a good husband."

"Oh, you can tell that from across the room?" I ask,
wondering how it is she can forget that when we had
trouble getting rid of my last husband, she shot him.
"Besides being ten minutes away from death if he

actually eats all that steak, he's twenty years too old for me and—shallow woman that I am—twenty pounds too heavy. Besides, I am *so* not looking for another husband here. I'm looking to design a new image for this place, looking for some sense of ambience, some feeling, something I can build a proposal on for them."

My mother studies the man in the corner, tilting her head, the better to gauge his age, I suppose. I think she's grimacing, but with all the Botox and Restylane injected into that face, it's hard to tell. She takes another bite of her steak salad, chews slowly so that I don't miss the fact that the steak is a poor cut and tougher than it should be. "You're concentrating on the wrong kind of proposal," she says finally. "Just look at this place, Teddi. It's a dive. There are hardly any other diners. What does *that* tell you about the food?"

"That they cater to a dinner crowd and it's lunchtime," I tell her.

I don't know what I was thinking bringing her here with me. I suppose I thought it would be better than eating alone. There really are days when my common sense goes on vacation. Clearly, this is one of them. I mean, really, did I not resolve less than three weeks ago that I would not let my mother get to me anymore?

What good are New Year's resolutions, anyway?

Mario approaches the man's table and my mother studies him while they converse. Eventually Mario leaves the table with a huff, after which the diner glances up and meets my mother's gaze. I think she's smiling at him. That or she's got indigestion. They size each other up.

I concentrate on making sketches in my notebook and try to ignore the fact that my mother is flirting. At nearly seventy, she's developed an unhealthy interest in members of the opposite sex to whom she isn't married.

According to my father, who has broken the TMI rule and given me Too Much Information, she has no interest in sex with him. Better, I suppose, to be clued in on what they aren't doing in the bedroom than have to hear what they might be doing.

"He's not so old," my mother says, noticing that I have barely touched the Chinese chicken salad she warned me not to get. "He's got about as many years on you as you have on your little cop friend."

She does this to make me crazy. I know it, but it works all the same. "Drew Scoones is not my little 'friend.' He's a detective with whom I—"

"Screwed around," my mother says. I must look shocked, because my mother laughs at me and asks if I think she doesn't know the "lingo."

What I thought she didn't know was that Drew and I actually tangled in the sheets. And, since it's possible she's just fishing, I sidestep the issue and tell her that Drew is just a couple of years younger than me and that I don't need reminding. I dig into my salad with renewed vigor, determined to show my mother that Chinese chicken salad in a steak place was not the stupid choice it's proving to be.

After a few more minutes of my picking at the wilted leaves on my plate, the man my mother has me nearly engaged to pays his bill and heads past us toward the back of the restaurant. I watch my mother take in his shoes, his suit and the diamond pinkie ring that seems to be cutting off the circulation in his little finger.

"Such nice hands," she says after the man is out of sight. "Manicured." She and I both stare at my hands. I have two popped acrylics that are being held on at weird angles by bandages. My cuticles are ragged and there's marker decorating my right hand from measuring carelessly when I did a drawing for a customer.

Twenty minutes later she's disappointed that he managed to leave the restaurant without our noticing. He will join the list of the ones I let get away. I will hear about him twenty years from now when—according to my mother—my children will be grown and I will still be single, living pathetically alone with several dogs and cats.

After my ex, that sounds good to me.

The waitress tells us that our meal has been taken care of by the management and, after thanking Mario, the owner, complimenting him on the wonderful meal and assuring him that once I have redecorated his place people will be flocking here in droves (I actually use those words and ignore my mother when she rolls her eyes), my mother and I head for the restroom.

My father—unfortunately not with us today—has the patience of a saint. He got it over the years of living with my mother. She, perhaps as a result, figures he has the patience for both of them, and feels justified having none. For her, no rules apply, and a little thing like a picture of a man on the door to a public restroom is certainly no barrier to using the john. In all fairness, it does seem silly to stand and wait for the ladies' room if no one is using the men's room.

Still, it's the idea that rules don't apply to her, signs don't apply to her, conventions don't apply to her. She knocks on the door to the men's room. When no one answers she gestures to me to go in ahead. I tell her that I can certainly wait for the ladies' room to be free and she shrugs and goes in herself.

Not a minute later there is a bloodcurdling scream from behind the men's room door.

"Mom!" I yell. "Are you all right?"

Mario comes running over, the waitress on his heels. Two customers head our way while my mother continues to scream.

I try the door, but it is locked. I yell for her to open it and she fumbles with the knob. When she finally manages to unlock and open it, she is white behind her two streaks of blush, but she is on her feet and appears shaken but not stirred.

"What happened?" I ask her. So do Mario and the waitress and the few customers who have migrated to the back of the place.

She points toward the bathroom and I go in, thinking

it serves her right for using the men's room. But I see nothing amiss.

She gestures toward the stall, and, like any self-respecting and suspicious woman, I poke the door open with one finger, expecting the worst.

What I find is worse than the worst.

The husband my mother picked out for me is sitting on the toilet. His pants are puddled around his ankles, his hands are hanging at his sides. Pinned to his chest is some sort of Health Department certificate.

Oh, and there is a large, round, bloodless bullet hole between his eyes.

Four Nassau County police officers are securing the area, waiting for the detectives and crime scene personnel to show up. They are trying, though not very hard, to comfort my mother, who in another era would be considered to be suffering from the vapors. Less tactful in the twenty-first century, I'd say she was losing it. That is, if I didn't know her better, know she was milking it for everything it was worth.

My mother loves attention. As it begins to flag, she swoons and claims to feel faint. Despite four No Smoking signs, my mother insists it's all right for her to light up because, after all, she's in shock. Not to mention that signs, as we know, don't apply to her.

When asked not to smoke, she collapses mournfully in a chair and lets her head loll to the side, all without mussing her hair.

Eventually, the detectives show up to find the four patrolmen all circled around her, debating whether to administer CPR, smelling salts or simply call the paramedics. I, however, know just what will snap her to attention.

"Detective Scoones," I say loudly. My mother parts the sea of cops.

"We have to stop meeting like this," he says lightly to me, but I can feel him checking me over with his eyes, making sure I'm all right while pretending not to care.

"What have you got in those pants?" my mother asks him, coming to her feet and staring at his crotch accusingly. "*Baydar?* Everywhere we Bayers are, you turn up. You don't expect me to buy that this is a coincidence, I hope."

Drew tells my mother that it's nice to see her, too, and asks if it's his fault that her daughter seems to attract disasters.

Charming to be made to feel like the bearer of a plague.

He asks how I am.

"Just peachy," I tell him. "I seem to be making a habit of finding dead bodies, my mother is driving me crazy and the catering hall I booked two freakin' years ago for Dana's bat mitzvah has just been shut down by the Board of Health!"

"Glad to see your luck's finally changing," he says, giving me a quick squeeze around the shoulders before turning his attention to the patrolmen, asking what they've got, whether they've taken any statements, moved anything, all the sort of stuff you see on TV, without any of the drama. That is, if you don't count my mother's threats to faint every few minutes when she senses no one's paying attention to her.

Mario tells his waitstaff to bring everyone espresso, which I decline because I'm wired enough. Drew pulls him aside and a minute later I'm handed a cup of coffee that smells divinely of Kahlúa.

The man knows me well. Too well.

His partner, whom I've met once or twice, says he'll interview the kitchen staff. Drew asks Mario if he minds if he takes statements from the patrons first and gets to him and the waitstaff afterward.

"No, no," Mario tells him. "Do the patrons first." Drew raises his eyebrow at me like he wants to know if I get the double entendre. I try to look bored.

"What is it with you and murder victims?" he asks me when we sit down at a table in the corner.

I search them out so that I can see you again, I almost say, but I'm afraid it will sound desperate instead of sarcastic.

My mother, lighting up and daring him with a look to tell her not to, reminds him that *she* was the one to find the body.

Drew asks what happened *this time*. My mother tells him how the man in the john was "taken" with me, couldn't take his eyes off me and blatantly flirted with both of us. To his credit, Drew doesn't laugh, but his smirk is undeniable to the trained eye. And I've had my eye trained on him for nearly a year now.

"While he was noticing you," he asks me, "did *you* notice anything about him? Was he waiting for anyone? Watching for anything?"

I tell him that he didn't appear to be waiting or watching. That he made no phone calls, was fairly intent on eating and did, indeed, flirt with my mother. This last bit Drew takes with a grain of salt, which was the way it was intended.

"And he had a short conversation with Mario," I tell him. "I think he might have been unhappy with the food, though he didn't send it back."

Drew asks what makes me think he was dissatisfied, and I tell him that the discussion seemed acrimonious and that Mario looked distressed when he left the table. Drew makes a note and says he'll look into it and asks about anyone else in the restaurant. Did I see anyone who didn't seem to belong, anyone who was watching the victim, anyone looking suspicious?

"Besides my mother?" I ask him, and Mom huffs and blows her cigarette smoke in my direction.

I tell him that there were several deliveries, the kitchen staff going in and out the back door to grab a smoke. He stops me and asks what I was doing checking out the back door of the restaurant.

Proudly—because, while he was off forgetting me, dropping by only once in a while to say hi to Jesse, my son, or drop something by for one of my daughters that he thought they might like, I was getting on with my life—I tell him that I'm decorating the place.

He looks genuinely impressed. "Commercial customers? That's great," he says. Okay, that's what he *ought* to say. What he actually says is "Whatever pays the bills."

"Howard Rosen, the famous restaurant critic, got her the job," my mother says. "You met him—the good-looking, distinguished gentleman with the *real* job, something to be proud of. I guess you've never read his reviews in *Newsday*."

Drew, without missing a beat, tells her that Howard's reviews are on the top of his list, as soon as he learns how to read.

"I only meant—" my mother starts, but both of us assure her that we know just what she meant.

"So," Drew says. "Deliveries?"

I tell him that Mario would know better than I, but that I saw vegetables come in, maybe fish and linens.

"This is the second restaurant job Howard's got her," my mother tells Drew.

"At least she's getting *something* out of the relationship," he says.

"If he were here," my mother says, ignoring the insinuation, "he'd be comforting her instead of interrogating her. He'd be making sure we're both all right after such an ordeal."

"I'm sure he would," Drew agrees, then looks me in the eyes as if he's measuring my tolerance for shock.

Quietly he adds, "But then maybe he doesn't know just what strong stuff your daughter's made of."

It's the closest thing to a tender moment I can expect from Drew Scoones. My mother breaks the spell. "She gets that from me," she says.

Both Drew and I take a minute, probably to pray that's all I inherited from her.

"I'm just trying to save you some time and effort," my mother tells him. "My money's on Howard."

Drew withers her with a look and mutters something that sounds suspiciously like "fool's gold." Then he excuses himself to go back to work.

I catch his sleeve and ask if it's all right for us to leave. He says sure, he knows where we live. I say goodbye to Mario. I assure him that I will have some sketches for him in a few days, all the while hoping that this murder doesn't cancel his redecorating plans. I need the money desperately, the alternative being borrowing from my parents and being strangled by the strings.

My mother is strangely quiet all the way to her house. She doesn't tell me what a loser Drew Scoones is—despite his good looks—and how I was obviously drooling over him. She doesn't ask me where Howard is taking me tonight or warn me not to tell my father about what happened because he will worry about us both and no doubt insist we see our respective psychiatrists.

She fidgets nervously, opening and closing her purse over and over again.

"You okay?" I ask her. After all, she's just found a dead man on the toilet and tough as she is that's got to be upsetting.

When she doesn't answer me I pull over to the side of the road.

"Mom?" She refuses to meet my eyes. "You want me to take you to see Dr. Cohen?"

She looks out the window as if she's just realized we're on Broadway in Woodmere. "Aren't we near Marvin's Jewelers?" she asks, pulling something out of her purse.

"What have you got, Mother?" I ask, prying open her fingers to find the murdered man's ring.

"It was on the sink," she says in answer to my dropped jaw. "I was going to get his name and address and have you return it to him so that he could ask you out. I thought it was a sign that the two of you were meant to be together."

"He's dead, Mom. You understand that, right?" I ask. You never can tell when my mother is fine and when she's in la-la land.

"Well, I didn't know that," she shouts at me. "Not at the time."

I ask why she didn't give it to Drew, realize that she wouldn't give Drew the time in a clock shop and add, "…or one of the other policemen?"

"For heaven's sake," she tells me. "The man is dead, Teddi, and I took his ring. How would that look?"

Before I can tell her it looks just the way it is, she pulls out a cigarette and threatens to light it.

"I mean, really," she says, shaking her head like it's my brains that are loose. "What does he need with it now?"

nocturne™

**WAS HE HER SAVIOR
OR HER NIGHTMARE?**

HAUNTED
LISA CHILDS

Years ago, Ariel and her sisters were separated for
their own protection. Now the man who vowed
revenge on her family has resumed the hunt, and
Ariel must warn her sisters before it's too late.
The closer she comes to finding them, the more
secretive her fiancé becomes. Can she trust the man
she plans to spend eternity with? Or has he been
waiting for the perfect moment to destroy her?

On sale December 2006.

SNHDEC

In February, expect MORE from

HARLEQUIN® Romance®

as it increases to six titles per month.

What's to come…

Rancher and Protector

Part of the
Western Weddings
miniseries

BY JUDY CHRISTENBERRY

The Boss's Pregnancy Proposal

BY RAYE MORGAN

Don't miss February's
incredible line up of authors!

www.eHarlequin.com

HRINCREASE

Romantic
SUSPENSE

**Excitement, danger and
passion guaranteed**

INTIMATE MOMENTS™

In February 2007
Silhouette Intimate Moments®
will become
Silhouette® Romantic Suspense.

Look for it wherever you buy books!

Visit Silhouette Books at www.eHarlequin.com   SIMRS1206

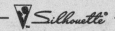

SPECIAL EDITION™

Silhouette Special Edition brings you a
heartwarming new story from the *New York Times*
bestselling author of *McKettrick's Choice*

LINDA LAEL MILLER

Sierra's Homecoming

Sierra's Homecoming
follows the parallel lives
of two McKettrick women,
living their lives in the
same house but
generations apart,
each with a special son
and an unlikely new
romance.

December 2006

Visit Silhouette Books at www.eHarlequin.com   SSESHIBC

Silhouette® Desire

**Don't miss
DAKOTA FORTUNES,**
a six-book continuing series following
the Fortune family of South Dakota–
oil is in their blood and privilege
is their birthright.

This series kicks off with
USA TODAY bestselling author
**PEGGY MORELAND'S
Merger of Fortunes**
(SD #1771)
this January.

Other books in the series:
BACK IN FORTUNE'S BED by Bronwyn James (Feb)
FORTUNE'S VENGEFUL GROOM by Charlene Sands (March)
MISTRESS OF FORTUNE by Kathie DeNosky (April)
EXPECTING A FORTUNE by Jan Colley (May)
FORTUNE'S FORBIDDEN WOMAN by Heidi Betts (June)

Visit Silhouette Books at www.eHarlequin.com SDPMMOF

REQUEST YOUR FREE BOOKS!

2 FREE NOVELS PLUS 2 FREE GIFTS!

✤ HARLEQUIN®

INTRIGUE®

Breathtaking Romantic Suspense

YES! Please send me 2 FREE Harlequin Intrigue® novels and my 2 FREE gifts. After receiving them, if I don't wish to receive any more books, I can return the shipping statement marked "cancel." If I don't cancel, I will receive 6 brand-new novels every month and be billed just $4.24 per book in the U.S., or $4.99 per book in Canada, plus 25¢ shipping and handling per book and applicable taxes, if any*. That's a savings of close to 15% off the cover price! I understand that accepting the 2 free books and gifts places me under no obligation to buy anything. I can always return a shipment and cancel at any time. Even if I never buy another book from Harlequin, the two free books and gifts are mine to keep forever.

182 HDN EEZ7   382 HDN EEZK

Name _____ (PLEASE PRINT) _____

Address _____ Apt. _____

City _____ State/Prov. _____ Zip/Postal Code _____

Signature (if under 18, a parent or guardian must sign) _____

Mail to Harlequin Reader Service®:

IN U.S.A.
P.O. Box 1867
Buffalo, NY
14240-1867

IN CANADA
P.O. Box 609
Fort Erie, Ontario
L2A 5X3

Not valid to current Harlequin Intrigue subscribers.

Want to try two free books from another line?
Call 1-800-873-8635 or visit www.morefreebooks.com.

* Terms and prices subject to change without notice. NY residents add applicable sales tax. Canadian residents will be charged applicable provincial taxes and GST. This offer is limited to one order per household. All orders subject to approval. Credit or debit balances in a customer's account(s) may be offset by any other outstanding balance owed by or to the customer. Please allow 4 to 6 weeks for delivery.

HI06

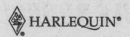
HARLEQUIN®

INTRIGUE®

COMING NEXT MONTH

#963 OPERATION: MIDNIGHT COWBOY by Linda Castillo
When agent-turned-cowboy Bo Ruskin is tasked to shelter
Rachael Armitage at his remote Wyoming ranch, nothing stays
hidden—not even this cowboy's damaging secret—as they're hunted
by a brutal crime lord.

#964 UNDER THE MICROSCOPE by Jessica Andersen
Investigator Maximilian Vasek suffers from damsel in distress syndrome.
So when his favorite damsel, Raine Montgomery, is targeted while
developing a medical breakthrough, he's going to have a hard time
breaking bad habits—and not hearts.

#965 SIX-GUN INVESTIGATION by Mallory Kane
The Silver Star of Texas
In the town of Justice, investigative reporter Anna Wallace is playing
havoc with Renaissance cowboy Zane McKinney's organized murder
investigation. But was what happened in the Justice Hotel all that odd
for a town with a history of violence?

#966 BEAST IN THE TOWER by Julie Miller
He's a Mystery
Dr. Damon Sinclair lives in his penthouse lab above Kansas City.
Thirty floors below, Kit Snow finds herself inexplicably drawn to this
shadowy man.

#967 THE BODYGUARD CONTRACT by Donna Young
Lara Mercer's latest mission: retrieve a lethal biochemical agent before
it's released into Las Vegas. But her backup is ex-lover Ian MacAlister, a
government operative taught that love and duty don't mix.

#968 THE AMERICAN TEMP AND THE BRITISH
INSPECTOR by Pat White
The Blackwell Group
When Max Templeton is assigned to lead the Blackwell Group, he
brings along his girl Friday Cassie Clarke to find the Crimson Killer—
Max's only unfinished case.